brazen

DANSBORO CROSSING
BOOK 3

AVERY SAMSON

Editor: My Brother's Editor

Cover Designer: Rachel Webb McCarthy

Cover Photo: CJC Photography

Models: Jered Youngblood & Jackie Coleman

contents

ELIOT

I'VE WALKED the straight and narrow for as long as I can remember. I got As in school, invested my money wisely, and chose a perfectly respectable, though boring, career. Good old accounting.

I can count the times my parents have been cross with me on one hand. I've never been sent to the principal's office or the dean's for that matter. I'm the perfect member of society, and I'm sick of it.

My younger sister, Austen, spent most of her life in one type of trouble or another. She spent half of her youth either sitting in the principal's office or grounded at home. Usually both. She was always one of the hottest topics of the rumor mill. And what does she have to show for it? A job she loves, a writing career that's taking off, and one of the sexiest boyfriends to ever walk the streets of Dansboro Crossing.

If that's not bad enough, Brontë, my youngest sister, got

pregnant from a one-night stand. She had to quit her burgeoning modeling career and move home. Her effort landed her a gorgeous billionaire who hunted her down and weathered the storm of emotions, only to propose marriage. She's also got the cutest baby on the planet to boot.

It's not that I'm jealous of them. Okay, maybe a little. At least in the boyfriend/fiancé department. I'll pass on the move home/baby department. It's just, as far as I know, no one has ever looked at me and thought *Hell yeah, I'll take the boring accountant with thighs a little too thick and unmanageable hair*. Life isn't fair like that. So, while they're both home snuggled up next to their happily-ever-afters, I'm out here going it alone.

Literally. I can't find anyone to help me, so I'm out here living it up on my own. Currently, I'm sitting in my car wondering if I've lost my mind.

In a month, I'll be thirty years old. As far as I can tell, my life is almost over and I've never really lived. I'm done with being plain old Eliot. Good, reliable Eliot. I'm ready to be crazy, fun Eliot.

That's what I was thinking anyway when I bought the "pyro pack" of fireworks from Sammy's Seismic Skyrockets. It seems like a pretentious name for around here, but who am I to judge? Sammy gave me a hell of a deal on the trunk load of fireworks.

"Okay, so here's to marking off number one on the list." I climb from my car. A nice, respectable, boring Toyota. I should add "buy a sports car" to the list. Would that make me too cliché? Maybe I'll just test drive a really fast sports car instead of buying it.

"God forbid you do anything on a whim, Eliot." Great, now I'm starting to talk to myself.

Popping the trunk, I heave one of the giant firecrackers that promises to both shoot off an impressive aerial display as well as a fountain of sparks out of the base. Setting it on the curb, I continue unloading until the trunk is empty.

I figure I have about ten minutes of fireworks to set off. At the last minute, I had Sammy add a handful of Roman candles to my purchase. I've always loved how they make me jump every time a new flame shoots out.

I check for traffic and lug one of the contraptions into the middle of the street. Dansboro Crossing has just one major road running to it with two bars, a couple of gas stations, and one restaurant which happens to be in one of the gas stations. Everything else is in town. There's usually not a lot of traffic in the evening out here.

A couple of kids made a huge splash setting fireworks off in the middle of the street when I was a junior in high school. The description that circulated through the hallways made it sound epic. Of course, I wasn't there. I was probably home studying for a test. Recreating it is first on my list.

Setting the fireworks down, I take out the long matches Sammy suggested and light the wick. It's glorious! The first one whirls sparks like a pinwheel before shooting several loud rockets into the air.

With a grin, I run quickly back into the street with the next set. Patrons from one of the bars filter out to watch.

The next firework I light has delayed rockets that burst forth, spraying the sky above us with different colors. The bar patrons applaud loudly as it shoots into the sky. Each successive firework gets bigger and bigger. The more I shoot off, the more people find a place to watch. I even have a couple of cars that pulled over to catch the show.

Sadly, all good things must end. When I finally place the

last and biggest one in the middle of the street, I have a grin on my face. I light it. It begins to whistle like a rocket. Each rocket that shoots from it vibrates deep in my chest.

I almost forgot the Roman candle in my back pocket. I pull it out and light it too. Something about this feels so freeing. This is what I've been missing. The rush of acting bad.

I'm standing in the middle of the road admiring my work when a siren blips behind me. Oh shit. I planned to be gone when any of the sheriff's department showed up to see what the fuss was about.

Spinning around, I find a patrol car parked behind me with a sheriff's deputy standing next to the door. A good-looking deputy. One I haven't seen before. I would remember him.

He has a scowl on his face, and his arms are crossed over his chest. He looks a little like one of the models on the covers of the western books I like to read. Yes, I like a good western. Sue me.

At least he does for about two seconds. Right up until I shoot him. Then it turns into an action movie. Or maybe *Walker, Texas Ranger*. The old ones; not the remake.

As if in slow motion, I watch in horror as one of the Roman candles fire right at him. I must have dropped my arm when I turned around. He leaps for the car but not fast enough for the rocket to miss completely.

I can't seem to do anything more than stand in the middle of the street with my mouth open. I'm almost positive I've just killed a man, a law enforcement officer at that. I literally shot the sheriff.

"Point that damn rocket up," he yells before easing back out of his car.

Instead, I manage to drop it on the ground. Now they're

shooting under the patrol car. It's not enough to shoot the sheriff, I'm going to blow his car up.

He throws the SUV into gear and backs away from the sparks. He climbs back out and snatches the Roman candle off the ground. It puffs out one more blast and dies.

"I'm so sorry," I try. I'm also trying not to laugh which doesn't help. I mean, come on. That was funny now that I know he's still alive.

"Get in the truck," he growls, cutting me off.

Holy shit, he's going to arrest me for attempted murder. I'm sure a good attorney can get it knocked down to assault with a deadly weapon, but still, I'm going to rot in jail for a very long time. All because he can't take a joke. Not because I'm a little too old to be shooting rockets in the middle of the street.

Opening the back door of his SUV, he glares at me until I climb inside. The bar patrons boo him, which makes his scowl deepen. I sit inside like a common criminal while he picks up the spent fireworks.

His mouth moves. I assume he's grumbling to himself as he hauls the old fireworks to the curb so no one runs over them. I was going to do that. My mid-life rebellion doesn't include endangering any of the local motorists.

When he has all the fireworks out of the street, he pulls my purse and keys out of my car before locking it. At least he's thoughtful. I'll remember that when I'm wasting away in a cell tonight. I wonder if I'll be the first person arrested in Dansboro Crossing for shooting a sheriff with a Roman candle.

He jerks open the driver's door, slides inside, and slams it shut again. Turning around, he glares at me sitting in the back seat.

"I really am—"

He holds up his hand and turns back around. So, a thoughtful dick. Okay. A sexy, thoughtful dick. I'm so dead.

We drive to the sheriff's office in silence. A myriad of thoughts flies through my brain on the way. Will I make friends in the big house? Which one of the characters in *Orange is the New Black* will I be? Does there need to be rope on my bath soap? Where do you still find that?

I hope my family finds me a good attorney. Someone under the age of eighty. Not that I have a problem with Mr. Truman, but I'm not sure he'll see the humor in this. He's never forgiven Austen for barfing in his mailbox. He dislikes all of us Caraways now because of association. Long story for another time.

I don't notice we're at the sheriff's office until the back door opens. He helps me out and, taking my upper arm, leads me inside. He sets me in a chair next to a desk. I won't point out that there's a big burn hole on the side of his uniform shirt. It's not lost on him. He inspects it before turning his glare back on me.

He has the most beautiful eyes. They're a deep brown like the color of dark chocolate as it melts or garden soil after a rain or even the café extreme at the Coffinated coffee shop near the courthouse. I might need to switch back over to straight westerns instead of the steamy cowboy romances I've been reading lately.

"Hey!" he says, making me jump. "I asked for your identification." He pushes my wallet to me.

Okay, so my assessment was right. He's a gorgeous dick. I pull my driver's license out from where it's tucked neatly in its designated slot. Maybe I should change that up too. Just throw it in my purse all willy-nilly. No, there's no reason to go completely around the bend. I hand it over and lean back in my chair waiting for the comments to begin.

"Your name's George?"

"Eliot! What are you doing here? I see you've met our new deputy, Owen." Sheriff Rogers walks out of his office to stand next to the desk. "Good Lord, Owen, what happened to your shirt?"

"Just an accident, sir," the new deputy says.

So his name is Owen. Not at all what I would have guessed. I was leaning more toward... Alejandro. Now that's a sexy name.

"I see. Well, get that shirt changed, officer. We don't want our local citizens to think we don't take pride in our office. Right, Eliot?" He winks at me and starts down the hallway. "Oh, and tell your folks I said hello. I look forward to seeing y'all on Sunday. Hey, Owen, why don't you plan on coming to church with us too."

Officer Owen looks at me with one eyebrow raised. "You're just the gift that keeps on giving, aren't you?"

He's right. Sheriff Rogers left no room in his statement for him to get out of the invitation to church. Standing with a derisive snort, he rips the uniform shirt off, slamming it down on the desk. The Kevlar follows, and then the T-shirt. Good Lord, I'm going to need church based on the thoughts racing through my head.

"Sweet Jesus!" I exclaim. The corners of his lips twitch. Is it possible he can smile? "I was talking about the giant burn mark on your side. Why wear Kevlar if it doesn't stop anything?"

I lower to my knees to inspect the burn etched into the skin at his waist. He lets out a small hiss when I tentatively run my fingertips over the skin surrounding the burn.

"Do you have any aloe vera?" I ask, looking up at him. It will at least take the burn out of it until he can have it looked at. He blinks once, looking down at me, then blinks again.

"It'll be fine." His voice seems deeper than it was.

"No, it won't. Oh, hang on, Cherylynn has one of the plants on her desk. I'll be right back." Hopping back up, I rush off down the hall to the dispatcher's office.

Cherylynn and I graduated together. We've been friends long enough to know exactly where she keeps the plant.

"Wait, Miss... Caraway," he calls after me.

"I'll be right back. Hold your horses."

I find the plant and return with a piece of it. Kneeling back down, I gently rub the sticky salve over the burn. I realize I've got my one hand spread over his abs for balance as I work. They are rock hard, and they tighten every time the aloe brushes his skin.

"Miss Caraway?" he growls.

Lord, give me strength.

"I grabbed a bandage while I was in there, so it won't get all over your shirt." Pulling it out of my back pocket, I smooth the large bandage over the burn. "There. You should probably have that looked at by someone." Looking back up, I'm met by eyes so dark brown I can't discern where the pupil ends and the iris begins.

"I'm sorry. It wasn't my intention to shoot you," I say, rising to my feet. My heart is like a hammer in my chest.

"What *were* your intentions?" he asks.

His voice is husky. It does nothing to stop the hammering. I shrug. I have no intention of explaining to anyone that I'm working through a list of regrets before I turn the ancient age of thirty.

"Is your name really George Eliot Caraway?"

"I wouldn't expect you to understand." Any of it, either

the name or my intentions. No one this good-looking would ever have regrets about things they were too scared to do when they were young.

"That you were named after the pen name of one of the most famous British authors of the Victorian era? Mary Ann Evans wrote such notable works as *The Mill on the Floss*, *Silas Marner*, and *Middlemarch* which is considered her greatest work." He gives me a smirk before moving to pull a clean T-shirt out of his bottom desk drawer.

I'm standing here like a fish with my mouth open staring at him. I'm not sure if it's because of his knowledge of the British novelist or, well, his abs.

"You'll get along great with my sister," I mumble.

"The librarian," he says like they're best friends.

"Of course." I don't have a problem with Austen. She's just everyone's best friend. The cool younger sister. Bleh.

"If you're going to throw me in jail, then do it so I can lay down. I'm getting tired." I cross my arms over my chest and refuse to meet his gaze. Because that's the mature thing to do. "I'll need to call my dad to bail me out." I can feel him studying me as he holds his shirt in his hand.

"Come on, I'll take you back to your car. But if I catch you doing anything like that again, I'll toss you in the back cells until morning."

Pulling his T-shirt on, he hands me my license. He motions for me to proceed with him down the hallway. We say goodbye to the other lone officer, and I feel a warm hand land on my lower back as he ushers me out the door.

"I can walk back, but thank you," I say. If he continues to touch me, I'll melt into a puddle. Please save me from becoming a swooning accountant. I'm not even sure that's possible.

"It's dark. I'll drive you back."

"What do you think happens here after dark?" I motion to the empty street in front of the sheriff's office. "Let me fill you in, Officer..." I didn't catch his last name. He's no longer wearing his nametag.

"Steele," he says, taking a step closer.

"What?" What were we talking about? Damn him for sending my senses into overload with his woodland scent.

"Owen Steele," he answers, patting his chest. "My name."

"Dick," I mumble.

"Owen," he reiterates, having clearly heard me. At least he has somewhat of a sense of humor.

"Let me tell you what happens around here after dark, Officer Steele."

"Owen."

"At least you know your name."

Now the corners of his mouth are starting to twitch. He must have me under his spell or something; I'm usually not quite this snarky.

"Nothing. Absolutely nothing happens here after dark. People just go to bed."

"So you're saying sex is all there is to do once it turns dark here?"

"I—well, no—I—I don't know. Don't put words in my mouth."

Oi. I feel heat spreading up my neck to my face. Why?! What's happened to the fierce, snarky Eliot from a second ago? I need her back.

Owen laughs. "Get in the car." He opens the passenger side door and waits for me to get inside.

As I see it, I have two options. I can act like a petulant

brat and walk anyway. Or I can swallow my annoyance and get in the SUV. I let out an impressive sigh. Then I climb into the passenger seat. He closes my door. I think I glimpse a smile as he walks around the front of the SUV. I wonder if it hurt.

two

OWEN

I TAKE my time crossing in front of the cruiser to the driver's door. Is it possible to be completely undone by a woman?

I was sitting at my desk filling out some paperwork when the first call came in. Some nut job was setting off fireworks in the middle of the street outside one of the handful of bars on the edge of town. Great, nothing like a drunk and disorderly at the end of a shift to make my night.

But that wasn't what I found when I arrived. Not exactly. What I found was a crimson-haired warrior standing in the middle of the street with fire shooting into the sky in front of her like in some action movie.

I stood there for a good five minutes just staring at her. Her long tresses floated around her in the breeze, and she had curves that made my mouth water.

And then she shot me with a damn Roman candle. It's not life-threatening, but it burns like hell. Then in the office, the memory of her on her knees in front of me, her soft touch caressing my body like a lover, my hand twitching to wrap in her long tresses was so strong it took my breath away.

Reaching the driver's door way too soon, I take a deep breath before opening it. She's sitting with her arms crossed over her chest staring out the passenger window. Her deep auburn hair flows over one shoulder like a siren's song pulling me under. Since when have I been so obsessed with hair?

Never in my thirty-four years have I had such a visceral reaction to someone. I haven't even gotten to her eyes, which are the color of bourbon. I can revisit that later tonight.

The whole changing shirts thing had been a complete middle school move. I work out religiously to stay in shape for my job. I know I have a decent body, but I've never blatantly tried to impress a woman with it.

"So why Eliot?" I ask, desperate to get my attention on something other than the problem growing below my belt.

"Why what, Eliot?" She spears me with those golden pools of amber. Great, I'm obsessing over her eyes now.

"No, I mean, why the name Eliot?"

"Oh." She looks out the front windshield. "My parents are both professors. My mom teaches literature, so we're named after novelists. There's also a real possibility they might have been high." I snort a laugh. That's something I've never done before. She smiles, making my heart race. "My younger sisters are Austen and Brontë."

"Wow, your mother must have been into British Victorian writers. Well, except Austen of course. She was Regency." I look over to find Eliot gaping at me. Do I tell her I've already worn out more library cards than I can remember? Or that I met her younger sister, Austen, the first day I moved to town?

"I guess it's better than being named after someone's grandpa," she snaps.

I should be offended. But it's hard to be when she bats her eyes at me. Even in derision.

"Mine, actually. I'm named after my grandpa Owen and my other grandpa Ambrose. You tell me what I should go with." She has the decency to blush. The pink creeping up her face just adds to her beauty, which in turn, adds to my growing problem. I need to get her out of my vehicle before I embarrass myself.

"I would definitely choose Owen. Though Ambrose has a certain appeal to it. At least it's better than Eliot."

"I like your name," I blurt out, much like a nervous teenager. I roll my eyes at myself. She pins me with her sultry, warm eyes again, and I fight not to blurt out everything I'm thinking. "It's unique."

"It is that," she answers. "Oh, this is me."

I pull the vehicle over to the curb as she throws open the door. Snatching up her wallet, she hops down. She turns around, her eyebrows knitted in concern.

"I really am sorry about shooting you. Not about the fireworks though. I needed to do that. You should get someone to look at that though. No need for it to become infected. Good night, Officer Steele."

Before I can get another word out, she closes the door, throws her long hair over her shoulder, and walks to her car. I watch her as she pops her trunk. Pulling out a garbage bag, she begins to clean up the remains of the fireworks.

"So you're a deviant with a conscience," I say, opening my door.

"What are you doing?" she asks.

"I'm helping you clean up." Squatting down, I pick up the remnants of one of the smaller rockets.

"You don't have to. It's my mess." I add the debris to her bag. I'm standing just a breath away, looking down at her. She has to be somewhere around five feet, eight inches. She would fit perfectly under my six-foot, two-inch frame. With heels on, she would be an easy reach when I pressed her up against a wall.

Jesus. When did I become so focused on sex? This is one of the citizens I'm sworn to protect. She shouldn't have to worry about protecting herself from me.

"I'm off duty with nowhere specific to go. I don't mind." That sounded pathetic. "Do you have anyone waiting for you at home?" Please stop talking. "Sorry, none of my business."

Spinning around, I walk into the street. Fortunately, the streets are pretty quiet this time of night, or I would have stood a good chance of being run over. I didn't even bother to check for cars. That's probably on page one of the training manual. I squat back down the furthest from her I can get to gather trash.

"I brought you a bag," she says next to me. I'm startled bad enough I rock down onto my knees and stick out a hand to prevent myself from falling the rest of the way.

I look up to where she's holding out a bag to me. I press back up to my knees while taking the bag from her hands. The breeze sends a hint of roses but also orange and jasmine. Fuck me, does she also have to smell like a wet dream?

"Thanks." I take the bag and try to focus on the task at hand. I can do this. I can focus on something other than how she smells. Or how her hair lifts off her long, supple neck every time the breeze blows. Or how good she'd look spread out in my bed.

"I think that about gets it," Eliot says, taking my bag. "Thanks for your help." She tosses the bags into her trunk and slams the lid closed. "Well, I'm sure I'll see you again."

I hold the door open as she slides into the driver's seat of her car. With a nod, I close it and watch her drive off. What did she mean? Does she want to see me again? Is she planning something else that I'll have to charge her with next time? Am I acting like a teenage girl analyzing every possible meaning behind her words?

With a frustrated groan, I close my eyes. My face tips toward the sky. A laugh reaches me from the closest bar. Hopefully, no one witnessed that brilliant act of manhood on my part. No reason to make myself fodder for the local gossip engine.

I unfist my hands and move to my vehicle. Why didn't I get her phone number? And then what? That feels like crossing a line.

I'll just wait. There's always a chance that she'll do something else marginally against the law and fall into my lap. Poor choice of words. Now all I can visualize is her on my lap.

I drop my head to the steering wheel, accidentally hitting the horn. I jerk my head back up and start the cruiser. There are only two things left to do tonight: a hot meal and a cold shower. Not necessarily in that order.

* * *

I keep my head down for the rest of the week. It takes all of my concentration to keep my mind off the crimson-haired beauty. I've been hired to do a job, and I'm bent on doing my best. Daydreaming won't earn me any accolades from the sheriff, and I want to keep this job.

I was a city cop for the first twelve years of my career. I responded to murders, participated in drug raids, helped investigate kidnappings, and worked to end all kinds of other debauchery. When my personal life spiraled apart, I welcomed the chance to start again in the small town of Dansboro Crossing.

So far most of my call-outs involve rowdy teenagers, Saturday night bar fights, and at least one missing cat. It was far from the adrenaline rush of the city, but the people seemed to be decent and I don't have to worry if I'll make it home at night.

"Hey, Owen," Cherylynn greets me, walking up to my desk. "We got a call that someone's climbed the water tower again."

"Do people do that often here?" I know about the water tower. It's hard to miss it looming over the town covered in purple and white with the school's mascot painted on it. It's not often you see a cougar that size. And why is it purple when they're normally tan?

At least it made more sense than the red and blue wampus cats in the next town over. I'm still trying to figure out what a wampus cat is. What's wrong with a simple bear or lion?

"Occasionally. It's usually just high school kids. Should I send the fire department?"

The fire department consisted of about twenty volunteers that have to come from their houses. I don't think that this is worth dragging them out of their evening routines for.

"I've got it. I'll call in when I see what the situation is if I need help." I slide my arms into my jacket and grab my keys. The water tower stands on the outskirts of town about ten minutes from the sheriff's office.

Pulling up to the bottom, I climb out of the SUV and look up. "Dispatch? I have the situation under control. No need for the fire department," I radio in.

"Copy that. Be careful. It's a long way to the top," Cherylynn responds.

"Roger." I hook my radio on my belt. I recognized the long, red hair blowing in the wind the moment I pulled up. Eliot is huddled on the top walkway. I can't tell if she's okay or not from the bottom. Since she's not making any moves to climb down, I guess I'm going up.

I sling the strap of a small first-aid kit over my chest and begin to climb.

"Hey," I say when I finally reach the top. "What are you doing up here?" I ease down the walkway until I'm squatting next to her. She's obviously cold, so I take my jacket off and slide it around her shoulders. I make a visual assessment of her, but nothing seems wrong.

"Naturally, it had to be you who showed up," she mumbles.

"Sorry?" Of course, she already hates me. I was a complete dick to her last time. I practically stripped naked, mentioned something about sex, and stared at her for a little too long.

"Nothing." She shakes her head as if to clear whatever thought had been there. "So, how far up do you think we are?"

"I would guess somewhere around one hundred and seventy feet. It's gorgeous up here."

"Oh god," she moans, shutting her eyes. It gives me a chance to study her unnoticed. She does appear a little paler than last time, and even in the cool breeze, she's starting to sweat. That could be a sign of practically anything.

"You're not on anything, are you?"

"Yeah, I'm a real tweaker." Her eyes pop open. "I barely take aspirin. Why would you think that?" She shoots a side-eye glare that sets my skin on fire. That's probably strike three for me.

"You seem jumpy."

"So you immediately went to drugs?" She snorts in derision and looks off into the distance. "It didn't occur to you that I might not like heights that much?"

"If you're scared of heights, why are you up here?"

"I didn't say I was scared," she snaps.

"Sorry." I hold up my palms in surrender. Her eyes flash in frustration right as the sun hits them, turning the irises into golden pools. They are the most stunning thing I've ever seen. Nothing in nature can rival them. I might be staring a little too long. "Why are you up here if you strongly dislike heights?"

"It was something I needed to do." Okay. That was the same answer she gave the other night. Was this some weird game? She stares off into space, ignoring me.

"Okay. Why don't we talk about it on the ground? Would you like me to escort you down?" I ask. I watch as she mulls it over. Obstinate doesn't even begin to describe her.

"Yes, please," she says finally, her shoulders sagging. "I would very much like to witness you acting like an escort."

I snort a laugh. Even terrified, her wit is still sharp as a tack. I stand and reach down to pull her up. When she's finally on her feet, she clings to me with a shiver. I would soak up her curves pressed against me if she wasn't so scared. Sorry, heavily disliking.

"Okay, here's what we're going to do. I'm going to get on the steps, and you're going to go with me. Don't look down. I'll be right here with you." She nods her head, still clinging to me. I back us to the ladder and take two steps down. "Come on. I've got you." I take a fist full of my jacket as she slowly eases down onto the step. "Now, nice and slow."

Together, we climb down the ladder one step at a time. I'm pressed against her as she shakily stays between me and the ladder. It's an awkward way to climb, but I don't want her to panic and fall. We reach the ground, and I'm forced to take a step back.

"Thank you," she says, suddenly throwing herself into my arms. Even with my jacket on, I can feel her breasts crushed against my chest. I would groan at the feeling, but that's way too pervy. "Sorry," she gushes, stepping back. "I must still be focused on the escort thing."

"My pleasure." Well, that sounded just as bad as a moan. "I mean, I'm happy to do it." Nope. "Er-I was happy to serve." For the love of God, stop talking.

"Are you going to arrest me this time?"

"For climbing a water tower? No, I don't think there was any harm done." Not until I imagine her breast pressed against me in the shower later. "You know, my shift just ended. Do you need something hot to drink? Warm you up? Coffee maybe?"

"Oh, no. I have plans. Here." She shakes out of my jacket and hands it back to me. "Thanks again." With a quick wave, she climbs in her car and drives away.

"You are such an idiot," I moan. I lean over the hood of my SUV until I can rest my head on it. "A perverted idiot."

three

ELIOT

I PANICKED. I know it. The water tower knows it. All those tiny woodland creatures know it. I agreed to dinner tonight with my family, but they would have understood if I'd texted that I had a dinner date with the gorgeous new deputy. But nope, I panicked. I'm sure he was only trying to be nice.

Maybe it wasn't a date, just a pity dinner. That makes me feel a little better. Now I feel justified in shutting him down. Besides, why would he want to ask me out? Better not start down a road that will only lead to disappointment. There's bound to be a line a mile long ready to entice the hot, new man in town.

"Hey," I yell, walking through the front door of my childhood home.

"We're in the kitchen, sweetie," Mom calls. I kick off my shoes by the door and walk down the hallway to the kitchen. It's where we always congregate.

We all get together several times a month for dinner in

various capacities. Sometimes, we eat at one of the local diners; others, we meet at my parents' house. Mom's cooking is always the best.

"What can I do to help?" I ask, popping a piece of celery from the cutting board into my mouth.

"I'm going to chop your fingers off if you do that again. Do you know how hard this is?" My youngest sister waves the knife at me. Brontë is standing at the island, knife in one hand, baby in the other.

"At least give me that baby." Brontë happily hands me my nephew. Brontë and her husband, Rand, made the most adorable baby I ever remember seeing. I'm not a bit partial. I blow bubbles on his stomach before settling him on my hip. "What did baby Keats do today?"

Because it wasn't bad enough growing up with the name Brontë, my sister had to saddle her son with the name Keats. I roll my eyes involuntarily thinking about it.

"I saw that," Brontë snarls.

"Guess what rumor I heard?" Austen rings out, entering the kitchen. Her fiancé, Reed, follows close behind with a grin on his face.

Reed was one of my best friends through high school. With his surfer good looks, I would have given my teeth to date him. But he only had eyes for my little sister.

"I heard a certain someone was seen getting out of the new deputy's car." Why does everyone always sing when they have gossip to impart? Is it an attempt to make it less cringe-worthy?

"Who?" Brontë asks as if the fate of the world rests on the answer. This house never lacks for drama when my sisters are in it.

"This person," Austen sings, pointing at me.

"Oh, my god, he is so hot!" Brontë twitters.

"Hey!" Rand chooses that moment to wander into the kitchen to grab him and Dad another beer.

"Good thing you put a ring on it, babe," she says, giving him a peck on the cheek. With a lazy grin, he disappears back into the family room with Reed trailing behind.

"I also heard they were seen locked in an embrace under the water tower." Austen wiggles her eyebrows.

"By whom? Who the hell was there?" Crap, that was the wrong thing to say. It's important to never admit to anything in front of those two. They might both be adults now, but that doesn't mean they act like it.

"Busted!" my sisters both exclaim together.

"What's his name?" Brontë asks.

"Officer Steele." They both stare at me, waiting for more. Finally, I roll my eyes. "Owen."

"Ooo, Owen," they tease. Such idiots.

"Oh, my god, how old are y'all?" I grouse.

"Girls, leave your sister alone," Mom says, pulling a pie out of the oven. "I can't believe I still have to say that."

"Hey, we're just returning the favor. I believe Eliot's advice to me when I was having my mental breakdown over Reed was 'Maybe you should find out what else that tongue can do' or something like that," Austen replies. It's true; I did say that.

"Yeah, and I was told it wasn't like I could get any more pregnant. I might as well ride him like there's no tomorrow," Brontë added.

I said that too. I'm just a fountain of good advice.

"And you both did," I say. "Because you're both dirty hoes."

"George Eliot Caraway!" Mom threatens. "No wonder the men hide in the other room."

"They started it." I stick my tongue out at my sisters and receive matching grins in response.

To an outsider, we might appear to be at odds with each other. But that's the farthest thing from the truth. I adore them both. I have since they came home from the hospital. There isn't a thing we won't do for one another.

I fought hard to drag both of my sisters, kicking and screaming, toward their happily-ever-afters. I believe in happy endings, even if I've never found mine.

"Did I hear someone just call my fiancé a dirty hoe?" Reed asks, sauntering into the kitchen. He leans against the island and enters a battle with Brontë over a piece of carrot. Austen points at me. "Damn, El, don't give away all of our secrets." Austen swats him with the towel she's holding.

"Out!" She points at the door he wandered in from.

"Wait, Reed, take that to the table." Mom points at a large casserole dish containing cheesy potatoes.

"Alright, but I can't promise there'll be any left for the rest of you." With a grin that seems to be permanently etched on his face since convincing Austen they belong together, Reed grabs two hot pads and leaves with the dish.

"Okay, girls, everybody grab something. Let's go eat." Mom leads us into the dining room carrying a large platter of roast beef. The men join us, and soon, everyone is busy passing plates around the table.

Secretly, I love our family dinners. They used to be every week on Sunday after church, but with Mom and Dad slowing down, they're more often than not on a weekday. They usually spend the weekend traveling now.

I make a mental note to discuss with my sisters rotating the dinners to give Mom a break. We all have our own houses now. Austen moved in with Reed at the end of the block, Brontë and Rand live in a large home he had remodeled across town, and I purchased my small home three years ago.

"So did anybody else hear about Eliot in a liplock with the new deputy at the water tower?" I still love my sisters, but Brontë has to die now. I open my mouth to correct the announcement when I'm cut off.

"Wow, that was fast. Didn't he just move into town a couple of weeks ago?" Rand asks.

"I think he rented the garage apartment from the Arnetts around the first of the month. Rumor is he was some hotshot cop from Chicago, moved here for personal reasons," Reed chips in.

"You know, he did have an Illinois driver's license when he applied for his library card. He brought in his rental agreement to prove he lived here," Austen adds. They already know more than I do, and I'm the one in the supposed liplock.

"I wonder what the personal reason was," Dad murmurs. He likes nothing better than a good mystery. And a good scandal. Just as long as we're not involved. Poor man's had a lot to deal with this last year.

"Do you think he's planning on staying?"

"I've also heard there is a path of single women lining up at his door."

"Yeah, but Eliot's already slipped inside."

"Or it's the other way around."

"Do you think he's left his wife and is in hiding?" Dad guesses. Yes, because working for the sheriff's office would be the best way to lay low. I roll my eyes. He has got to stop watching Hallmark Mysteries. "Eliot, are you sneaking around with a married man? Maybe we shouldn't go this weekend, Elise."

I've heard enough. Slapping both palms on the table, I

push to my feet.

"First, Officer Steele was nice enough to help me down from the water tower is all. Second, if I want to 'lock lips,' dry hump, or suck off the new guy, that's my business. I'm twenty-nine, for Christ's sake. Why would you cancel your vacation over this? And finally, wouldn't he be working as the local baker if he was in hiding?"

That could be one of my best outbursts. It was glorious. Except everyone is staring at me. Why does no one ever get my humor?

"I'll get her," Rand says quietly when the baby starts to cry upstairs. Oh.

"Now, if you're done discussing my non-existent sex life, I'm going to pass on dessert and head home where I will polish off a bottle of wine and pass out in my bed. Alone." I turn to storm from the room but remember my manners. "Thanks for dinner, Mom. Have fun on your trip." I kiss her on the cheek and set my plate in the kitchen before leaving.

I make it halfway down the sidewalk when I hear Austen chasing after me. "Wait, Eliot." Austen catches up to me at the car. "Are you okay? You know we're just teasing you, right?"

"I'm fine, and of course, I know you're just jacking with me. I have been your sister for a long time now, right?" Austen pulls me into a hug. I'm not huge on them, but I make an exception this time.

"We just want it to be your turn to be happy. Man or no man."

"Men," I say, rolling her eyes. "Can't live with them—"

"—can't get the good dick without them," Austen finishes with a grin.

"I taught you well, grasshopper." With one last hug,

Austen bounces back toward the door. "I'm trying to be happy," I whisper. "I really am trying."

* * *

I sit hunched over my desk in my tiny office working on the funeral home's profit and loss statement. Did I mention I have my own accounting firm? It's just me, but I like it that way. It makes the gossip around the water cooler much tamer. Sometimes, though, it can get a little boring. Like doing the P & L for a funeral home.

The Slayed family had been pioneers when the town of Dansboro Crossing was founded. However, I'm not sure about using the family name for their business, even if they have been handing it to the next generation for over one hundred years.

Still Slayed Mortuary is one of my top clients, so I do whatever is necessary to meet their accounting needs. If only Dad wouldn't mumble "You stab 'em, we slab 'em" every time we drive by their business.

I'm trying not to think about what falls under the category "chemicals" when I feel the air in the room shift. Looking up, I find him standing at the door glaring at me.

It only takes me a moment to take in all that glorious muscle standing in my office before my gaze returns to his face. He seems tenser than the last time we met. This doesn't bode well.

"Sheriff Steele. What can I help you with today?" I'm positive he's not here because he needs his expenses placed in the proper categories. By the look on his handsome face, I'd say he has something else in mind. He reaches into a sack I didn't notice until just now and holds up a can of spray paint. He shakes it at me.

"What's that?" There are three choices when cornered with an accusation: deny everything, make it look like their fault, or beg forgiveness. You always try to get away with it first. If that doesn't work you can try to act indignant. If all else fails, cry. I'm going with the first one. I cock my head and try to look perplexed.

He lowers his eyes into a squint and tosses the can into my trash. Pulling out another can, he repeats the motion while he waits for me to speak. Poor man, he has no idea I'm the queen of denial. By the fourth can, it's obvious he's lost his patience.

"You can't prove those are mine." I can tell he's not buying the innocent act. The ringing noise my metal trash can is making is a pretty good clue. I silently curse myself for forgetting the stupid cans in the bushes. Very environmentally unfriendly of me.

He raises one eyebrow and crosses his arms over his chest. His biceps bulge in his uniform. How does he make khaki look so sexy? I bet his thighs bulge inside those slacks too. Maybe something else bulges too. Yeah, you flex that thing, baby. Why is he scowling at me? What are we talking about?

"There are three giant letters on the street in front of the school. G. E. C. Who do you think they belong to?" he growls. Oh, that's right. Spray paint.

"Hmmm." I tap my finger against my chin in concentration.

"Yeah, that's what I thought." He runs his strong hands through his hair, making it stand up in all the right directions. Because he isn't sexy enough already. Craptastic. I need to get whatever raging hormones I've kicked into high gear under control. "At least tell me one thing. Are you working your way up to a felony?"

I snort a laugh, and he seems to relax a little. "Felonies. I spit in the face of felonies." Jesus, I'm a dork.

"Okay. That's something I guess. Listen, as much as I enjoy chasing you around, I do have a real job to do." His deep-brown eyes meet mine. I think I could drown in them. "Like finding Mrs. Holcomb's cat. Again."

"That cat's a menace. Just leave some tuna on her back porch, and he'll show up in a hurry."

"Thanks." I wait for him to say more, but he just stands there. Is he debating the cost of tuna? He's starting to freak me out.

"Was there something else?" I ask.

"Oh, um, no, I guess not. Just... stay out of trouble."

"Aye, Captain." I give him the stupidest fake salute possible. He doesn't turn to leave. He doesn't do anything. Finally, as if shaking himself out of a daze, he backs out the door. I wasn't going to shoot him in the back with a fire- cracker if that's what he was thinking. He could have just walked out like a normal person.

"Um, are you busy?" he asks, popping his head back around the doorjamb. It startles the hell out of me.

"Of course I'm busy. It's the end of the month. I'm buried in paperwork." That came out much bitchier than I intended it to. "Sorry."

"No, I understand. I can imagine how much more work there is for you at the end of the month. Maybe tonight you can get some extra sleep instead of, you know, painting the street in front of the school." I look up to be met with a bril- liant smile. Wow. I want to eat those dimples for lunch. Okay, that sounded creepy to me too.

"I confess to nothing," I answer, hoping the smile on my face convinces him I'm not as awkward as I feel. His eyes lock with mine for just a moment before he sighs.

"Well, I'll get out of your hair. Have a good evening, Eliot."

"You too, officer."

"Owen." With one last smile, he disappears down the hall. Wait, come back. I sigh deeply and bend back over my computer screen. No use lusting after the new beefcake in town. Someone is bound to snatch him off the market soon, and I'm not fooling myself into believing it will be me.

I have better things to think about anyway. Pulling a small notebook out of my desk, I turn to the first page. Taking my pen, I mark through the line that reads "Spray paint the street in front of the high school."

Checking the next line, I debate if I can get it in this weekend. Why not? I'm free tomorrow night, might as well get on with it. I smile as I store the notebook back in my desk. That will make four behind me. At this rate, I'll work my way through all of it before my deadline—my thirtieth birthday.

four

OWEN

WAS THAT STRIKE TWO? Am I even up to bat yet? I didn't get the words out this time before she struck me down. I don't remember being this bad with women. In the past, I simply said "Let's have dinner," and nine out of ten times, they said yes. Okay, maybe seven out of ten times. But still, it wasn't this hard.

"Can I help you find something?" I jump, hearing a whispered voice behind me. Spinning around, I come face to face with the head librarian. "Officer Steele, right?"

"Please, call me Owen. I'm just trying to find something to read this weekend."

"Oh? No plans then?"

"No. No plans. I tried, but I was shot down."

She nods sagely. "Yeah, she can be clueless like that."

"How do you even know who I'm talking about?"

"Please." She laughs. "You moved to a very small town. Everyone knows everything around here, possibly even before you do." I scowl at her, and she laughs again. "Don't worry, you'll get used to it. Sometimes," she adds, leaning in as if she was plotting something sinister, "you can even use it to your advantage if you know how to work it right." She leans back, flashing a grin. "Alright, let's see what we can find to keep you company tonight."

She turns and starts down the aisle, looking through the stacks. I shake my head in exasperation before following. Are all of the Caraway women this crazy? The two I've met so far are both beautiful and smart, but they're as confusing as a goat on Astroturf. I'm not sure I used that right. I just heard that line earlier at the office and decided it was a keeper.

This town is full of idiosyncrasies I've discovered. The gossip I can do without, but I enjoy seeing the same people around town and being greeted by name. The fact that Austen seems to know enough about me to pull book suggestions that I want to read both fascinates and disarms me. Maybe that's a recurring theme for the women in this town. Or maybe just Caraways.

With an armful of books, I follow Austen back up to the circulation desk. She chats away at me while checking out my books until a tall, blond man walks through the door. I watch her whole face light up. If only I could convince Eliot to look at me like that.

"Hey, babe."

"Hey," she responds. I stand awkwardly while they grin at each other. "Oh, Reed, this is Owen Steele."

"Ahh," Reed says, shaking my hand. "So, you're the new guy in town? I'm Reed Campbell. I hear you've been chasing my girlfriend's older sister around."

"Uhh" is all I manage to say. Has it already circulated that I've been shot down twice by Eliot? Or one and a half times. I'm not sure about that last one.

"Word has it your sister has turned into quite the hellion. I heard from Raffe, who heard from old man Robbins, that Owen here had to arrest Eliot for setting off fireworks in the middle of the street the other night," Reed continues.

"She did not!" Austen gasps.

She's laying it on a little thick. I'd be willing to bet she knew all about it before the first rocket went up.

"And her initials are painted the size of a school bus in front of the high school. Chad told me about that one. I kept telling y'all she'd crack one day." Turning toward me, Reed adds, "Eliot and I graduated the same year. She's been one of my best friends since...when, babe?"

"Mmm, freshman year?"

"Yeah, that sounds right. She's always been wound a little tight. It's about time she loosened up and let her hair down. Anyway, are you about ready to get some supper? I'm starving. You want to come?" I've been watching them like a tennis match. It takes a few minutes of them staring at me expectantly to realize the question was aimed at me.

"Oh, no thanks. I'm going to head home. It seems like I have a lot of reading to do." I wave one of the books.

"Okay, maybe another time. Hey, a couple of us have a poker group that plays once a month if you're interested in jumping in sometime. Just give me a call. You can find me around town most days," Reed says.

"Is there anything else I can help you find?" Austen asks.

"No, I'm good. Have a nice evening." With a nod at Austen and another handshake from Reed, I head toward my SUV. Setting the books on the passenger seat as I slide in. I watch the couple walk down the street to the small pizza place on the corner. I sigh as I start the truck. Pizza sounds good. I could always order one later while I'm reading.

I've finished the pizza, gotten a pretty good start on one of my new library books, and am brushing my teeth in the bathroom when I hear my phone ring. "Hello?"

"Owen, can you go over to Principal Hamby's and see what's going on? He reported someone lurking around his house. Ray's out busting up one of the high school parties at the rock crusher."

I learned when I first arrived that the rock crusher is the deep part of the river made when they dug out the rock needed to build the roads long ago. It has a cliff face where the kids jump off on one end and a beach-like area on the other. The kids liked to light a fire and hold parties on the sandy end.

"I hate to wake Sheriff Rogers."

"No, don't wake Wes. I'll go take care of it."

"Thanks, Owen." Cherylynn gives me the address and hangs up.

I pull on a pair of jeans and a T-shirt. A clean uniform shirt goes over the T-shirt. I don't see any reason to get too excited about being in full uniform for what most likely is a stray dog. Slipping on my boots, I grab my gun belt, Kevlar, and drive across town.

I pull in across the street of what looks like one of the nicer homes in town. Stepping from my cruiser, I shake my head at the scene in the front yard. Toilet paper hangs from every branch of the huge oak trees in the front yard. I can't decide if I should be pissed or impressed by the muscle it must have taken to throw the rolls that high.

Quietly, I close my car door. I lean against the front fender, my arms crossed, and watch as the voluptuous beauty with the riot of red hair rears back to let another roll fly. Based on what I can see, she's been here for a while. I'm certain there isn't a roll of toilet paper left at the grocery store.

When Eliot holds up both fists in triumph as a roll flies over the tree, I push off the car with a sigh. Walking up behind her, I wait until she spins around to grab another roll out of the package at my feet. She stops short with a squeal.

"We should really stop meeting like this," she says after recovering. Without a word, I wrap my hand around her upper arm and start for my truck. "You're not going to haul me in for a little redecorating, are you?" I stay silent as we reach the SUV. Opening the passenger door, I slide her onto the seat.

Walking back across the street, I snatch up the remaining bag of toilet paper. "Mr. Hamby?" I ask when a portly, balding man answers the door.

"Yes?"

"I'm with the sheriff's department. It looks like a couple of kids were up to no good. I didn't find any damage except for the exceptional amount of paper."

The principal thanks me, accepting the package as compensation. We agree that filing a report would be a waste of time. With a final good night, I leave him to clean up the mess.

Sliding into the driver's seat, I turn to stare at Eliot. She, in turn, never takes her eyes from the front windshield.

I can't decide what to do with her. I'm not taking her to the station for acting like a teenager, even if it is considered vandalism. I sit, debating as I thump the steering wheel with my thumbs. Finally, I slide the vehicle into gear and pull away from the curb.

"My car—"

"Nope," I say, cutting her off.

She doesn't get to push me off my game this time. When I head out of town, she finally turns to look at me.

"Are you taking me to your lair to chain me to the wall until you can turn me into a skin suit?"

"It's a thought."

We return to silence. After a twenty-minute drive, I pull up outside of an all-night truck stop in the next town. I turn off the engine and climb out. I don't bother to see if Eliot follows as I walk to the door of the diner. Stepping back, I hold it open until she walks through, her head held high. It's all I can do to stop the grin threatening to spread across my face. Damn woman.

She chooses a booth by the windows, sitting in the seat across from me. A young waitress hustles over to bring us menus.

"What would y'all like to drink?" she asks. I watch as Eliot looks over the menu with a sigh.

"Just some water," she says in resignation.

"Why don't you bring us some bacon cheese fries and two coffees," I say without taking my eyes off Eliot.

She opens her mouth to protest but quickly closes it when I raise an eyebrow in challenge. The waitress takes our menus, hurrying off to bring our coffee. Leaning back against the booth, I sling one arm over the back and study her.

"So you must think I'm crazy," she says. It's crossed my mind.

"Why do you say that?" I ask.

It seems more diplomatic than just agreeing. She looks up at me, her golden eyes meeting mine. She's so beautiful. For just a moment, I forget what we're talking about.

"I never get into trouble normally. It's just..." She looks

away. Her eyes fill with sadness. So much so that all I want to do is pull her onto my lap, hold her close, and assure her that whatever she's going through, I'm here every step of the way.

But several things stop me. We don't know each other that well, and I'm pretty sure she would hate being coddled. Also, I still have to enforce the law, and she's running through it as hard as she can.

"Just what? Because at this rate, you might just get a cell block named after you."

* * *

ELIOT

I don't know what he expects me to say. That I'm so colossal a loser that I've resorted to trying to relive my youth by wreaking havoc around town? Well, a better youth. I know nothing I'm doing makes sense to a sane person. And to be honest, I'm not even completely sure it makes sense to me.

I do know one thing though. I'm not sharing any of this with the man sitting across from me.

He doesn't say another word. He just dives into the fries while I sip my coffee and decide what to tell him.

"I'll make a deal with you," he finally says. His warm gaze meets mine. It almost makes me confess everything, but I stop myself just in time. "Promise me you won't do anything that will get you hurt, and I'll let it go. Again."

"I promise."

"I mean it. No rockets, no dangerous climbs, no breaking and entering, no grand theft auto."

"Grand theft auto?" I chuckle. "I promise I don't have

anything planned that will get me or anyone else hurt. Is that what you want to hear?" He searches my face, looking for something. I'm not sure what, but whatever it is, he must find it. He nods and looks back down at the plate.

"Okay," he says, nodding. "Okay."

"So, were you just sitting around hoping for someone to arrest?" He smiles, and I feel the tension ease some. "Or were you in the middle of preparing for a crazy night out?"

"I was getting ready for bed."

"At nine? How old *are* you?"

"Not all of us have such a busy social schedule." He rolls his eyes.

"Some social schedule. I spent the evening buying toilet paper and using it on my old principal's house. Not exactly my idea of a night out on the town."

"What is your idea of a night on the town?" he asks.

He settles against the back of the booth with his legs stretched into the aisle. His arm slides to the back of the seat again. His entire focus is on me. I don't think I've ever had a man so fully invested in what I'm about to say. It's almost unnerving.

"Well." What does it look like? "I don't know. Maybe dinner at a posh restaurant, then the latest hit on Broadway, followed by drinks with friends. I'd crawl into bed in the early morning, totally exhausted but feeling alive. I like to think of myself on the same level as a twenties flapper." I grin, but he just stares at me.

"Fine," I finally relent. "It doesn't matter as long as it's fun and the conversation is good. Food helps." I wave a fry at him. "Stupid, right?"

"No. It's not stupid. It sounds like a nice way to spend an evening. All I did this evening was pizza and a book. It was nice enough. Putting pants back on to pick up Dansboro Crossing's newest felon, though, was the icing on the cake."

"Putting pants on. What a tease."

"Yeah," he says with a wink. "I'd much rather be taking them off."

five

ELIOT

I DON'T EVEN KNOW what that was. Was it a sexual innuendo? Does he just not like pants? I've been asking these questions since he dropped me back off at my car two nights ago. Not much was said after the pants comment. I mean, what do you follow that up with?

I've kept a low profile since being busted for toilet papering the principal's house. Seems the least I can do. The sheriff's deputy really could use some rest. I think all that chasing me around has somehow fried his brain. Hence the pants comment.

"You've outdone yourself this time," Austen says, stepping into my office.

I've finished catching up on the funeral home books and have moved on to the coffee shop books. I'd much rather account for coffee beans than caskets.

"A work of true poetry," Brontë adds, following her through the door with Keats on her hip. "Where did you find your inspiration?"

"*Captain Underpants*. Where else?" I have all the books. Don't judge; I got them in elementary school.

"Can we assume the reference is to the bangin' new deputy in town?" Austen asks. "Do you think there'll be retribution?"

"Maybe a spanking."

"Brontë!"

"What? I'm just saying it wouldn't be the worst thing to happen to Eliot." That's my youngest sister. Keeping it classy.

"Did y'all just come to get in my way, or do you have something you want?" I ask.

"We're hungry," they whine at the same time.

"It's ten in the morning."

"It's called brunch, El."

I roll my eyes. I've had to put up with Austen's sass since she could talk. I should be angry with her. She did steal the hottest guy in my grade. But, I adore her.

"Where do you want to eat brunch, Aus?" Two can play the snark game.

"Since this will probably be your last meal as a free woman, anywhere you want," Brontë says.

"It's not that bad," I argue.

"It talks about his ass."

"In poetic form." It's a haiku actually. That's all the letters I had. Still, I think it's rather good, and he's an easy target. Not that I think about him or his ass all the time. Definitely not. Nope.

"Can we please go eat before this one wants to be fed again?" Brontë pleads.

"Yes, let's go." I grab my purse from my drawer. Ushering my sisters from my office, we decide to walk to brunch. There's only one place close that serves a full menu before eleven, and it's a block over.

When we reach The Hungry Heifer, we find it full of men. Most of them are the older retired crowd. But, there's a table made up of the banker, the attorney, the real estate guy, an insurance salesman, and one of the local ranchers. You want to do business in the middle of the workday in a small town? Find the coffee shop.

"How about the back booth?" I suggest.

We weave our way through the small diner. I sit on one side with Austen. Brontë and Keats slide into the other. My eyes roam the rest of the restaurant until I notice someone at one of the tables full of locals glaring back. It's the pastor from the First Baptist Church. Yeah, I hit several signs around town. This should be a lesson to him on securing your letter sign better.

"You're popular today," Austin says.

"Yeah, well, you're just jealous." She shakes her head and looks at the menu. I do the same. It's the same menu they've had since we were kids, but it's better than catching the glaring gaze of anyone else. I may have gone too far. It was on the list, though, so I was obligated. They'll get over it.

"We'll see what the deputy thinks when he discovers it," she adds. "He might not think you're so clever."

* * *

OWEN

Today started just like any other day as a deputy in a small town. I got to the office early by way of the coffee shop.

Left not soon after arriving to do a welfare check on one

of the elderly citizens. Turns out she was up watching a late-night movie and overslept her morning canasta club. I drank more coffee and ate a piece of her coffee cake before I was allowed to leave. Good thing I signed up at the local gym as soon as I arrived in town.

From there, I headed to one of the ranches to write up a report on a stolen deer blind. I explained to the irate hunter that I wasn't making any kind of caste of shoe impressions around something that could have disappeared any time between last night and three months ago. Life is not one big episode of *C.S.I.*

When I get back to the office, I'll put it in the system. If one randomly shows up, I guess it can now be identified from the other similar-looking one hundred others in the county.

"I guess if you've got it, use it," I'm greeted by one of the other deputies when I walk back through the sheriff's office door. The others snicker. Okay.

"She's not lying," Cherylynn adds.

"What are you talking about?" I ask.

"You mean you haven't seen it?"

"Seen what?"

"Owen," the chief bellows from his office before she gets the chance to answer. "March it in here."

The other deputies laugh again. Shit.

"Yes, sir?" I step into his office. He motions for me to close his door. Double shit.

"Now, son, I don't know exactly what's going on, but you need to get this nipped in the bud. It's just not professional. Nor is it the image of this sheriff's office we want to portray. How will the locals be able to take you seriously if they're too busy thinking about a poem to your backside?"

I'm going to kill her. "Why don't you head on over to the post office and get that dealt with?"

"Yes, sir." I open my mouth to try and apologize, but he's already back to reading through the reports on his desk. How do you apologize for something you haven't even seen yet anyway? "I'll get right on that."

He nods, and I leave his office.

"You know, it's not all bad. I wouldn't mind an ode or two to my ass," Arlo says as I march toward the door.

"And you can always use it to supplement your income. You already have a stripper uniform." Ray laughs. I hear them all laugh as the front door closes behind me.

I jump in my cruiser and make the short drive to the post office. There's a small crowd around the community bulletin board.

It's one of those small town typical ones. One side is a place to hang up garage sales, lost dogs, and general announcements with push pins. The other side is a board with white plastic letters inside a glass case that gives information about a major event. Like the Lion's Club pancake supper that used to be there.

The side with the push pins looks fine. The other side, however, is not. What used to be all the details for the pancake fundraiser is now a poem. A haiku, to be precise. About my ass. Three lines, seventeen words describing someone's backside. It's not necessarily mine.

His backside is fine.
Round, firm, like steel orbs I find.
They beg deputy.

"You know, it's not bad," someone says. "I would guess something Austen Caraway wrote since she's the only one with the writing chops."

"But why use the new deputy's bottom when she has the Campbell boy's for inspiration?" someone else points out.

"It could be about anyone," I try.

"No, it's you." Someone else laughs. "None of those other boys have had an ode about their butt on the bulletin board before. Not until you."

"Damn Eliot," I grumble.

"No. Can't be Eliot. You've got the wrong sister. That one is too straight and narrow for this."

"Straight and narrow, my ass." I hear the words leave my mouth too late to stop them. There's chuckling behind me. I squeeze my eyes shut for a moment in frustration. "Who has the key to this thing?"

"I do," a tiny woman announces. "I'm the postmistress, Lana."

"Lana, can you please change this back?"

"I can as soon as I get the other letters back."

"Other letters? You mean there are more of these signs?" I'm going to kill her. Eliot, not the postmistress.

"There are three others. One at the body shop, one at the library, and one at the Baptist church," she informs me. "I'll bet Pastor Greg is fit to be tied if his board is anything like this one. At least ours is PG-rated. I heard the body shop had a real humdinger."

"Okay," I say after a minute. "Can you please take this down, and I'll see to getting your letters back to you?" There's a rumble of disgruntlement from the crowd behind me. If they want to read more about my ass, they'll have to wait for the book.

"Are you sure that's what you want to do?" Lana asks.

"Yes." The word comes out a little too aggressively. I might be writhing in embarrassment, but that doesn't mean I can't sound professional. "Yes, please."

"You know it's against policy to take down a work of art without the council voting on it," someone behind me points out. Probably one of the councilmen. Everyone laughs.

"Just take it down," I order Lana through clenched teeth.

With a sigh, she opens the case and begins taking the letters down. There's a collective "Awww" from the crowd. As soon as she's done, I take the box of letters she hands to me and head back to my cruiser. I need to find the rest of the boards. Then I can kill Eliot.

The rest of the bulletin boards are not too bad. The one at the church is much tamer. Though the pastor is hopping mad about it.

The library's is inside the lobby. It's funny and geared to kids. Kim, at the circulation desk, tells me they've decided to leave it. My ass does not come into play, so I'm good with that.

The local body shop has already changed theirs back. They thought it was hilarious if not a little lewd for the local citizenry. I didn't even ask what it said.

By the time I return to the office, I've put together a plan in my head of restitution for Eliot. I have to make my way through more taunts to my desk.

I'm calling around to locate Eliot when Ron tosses a box of flyers I requested from him. He's president of the Lion's Club this year, and they're hoping to make the pancake supper bigger than ever. I have an idea of how to help with that.

"Thanks, Ron. I'll get these out."

"I appreciate it. Owen, right?"

We shake hands. He wanders off to visit with Wes in his office. It seems like everyone is friends with the chief. I need to get better at meeting the town. I don't want our first introductions to always be writing them a ticket.

I leave the office again, heading for the diner down the street. Sources tell me the Caraway sisters are just finishing up brunch. I should be able to interrogate... I mean, question Eliot there. With the box of flyers in tow, I push inside the diner. It takes me three seconds to scan the patrons before my gaze lands on her.

As angry as I am at her, I can't help but take a minute just to admire her beauty. Her long red hair is swept up in some form of a loose bun. The kind that seems both effortless and time-consuming at the same time. She throws back her head to laugh at something one of her sisters says, exposing her long neck, and I forget for a moment why I'm here.

"Do you need a table, deputy?"

"Oh," I answer, shaking myself out of my fantasy. There was a moment of imagined nakedness on her part in my vision, so I'm safe calling it that. "No, I see my quarry."

She gives me an odd look before I set off across the restaurant. The sisters' laughter stops when I reach the table.

"Uh-oh," Austen says, sizing me up. "I think I hear books begging to be shelved. Owen." She stands as I nod in greeting. "I'll see you later."

"Yeah, I'll go with you," Brontë adds, easing from the booth. "This little one is starting to smell funky. Good luck," she says over her shoulder as she follows Austen.

I watch as Austen and Brontë leave the diner. My gaze

turns slowly back to Eliot. She's looking up at me with her big golden eyes. Her eyelashes bat once, twice. The urge to run my hand into those fiery tresses is overwhelming, but the last thing I need is a public harassment suit. Also, who uses the word tresses? I need to back off the historical fiction for a while.

"Why, Deputy Steele. What a pleasant surprise." She smiles her thousand-watt smile. I slide into the booth across from her. Oh, this is going to be fun.

six

ELIOT

THIS SEEMS like cruel and unusual punishment if you ask me. Not the part about going door-to-door handing out flyers for the pancake breakfast. The part where I have to do it accompanied by a man with rippling muscles poured into a sheriff's department T-shirt and jeans that seem to be spooning that ass I waxed poetic about. I mean, what is up with the jeans? They should be issued a ticket for how they wrap around his thick thighs like a lover.

"Hello, Mrs. Cates," I say when the door I'm currently pounding on opens instead of considering the impressive ridge in the front of those jeans. Again.

"Hello, Eliot. What are you up to this evening? Would you like to come in?"

"No, no. I just wanted to remind you about the Lion's Club pancake breakfast coming up. This year, the money raised will go toward the refurbishment of the senior citizens center." I go on babbling about the needed remodel until Owen cuts in.

"I'd like to introduce myself. I'm Owen Steele, the newest addition to the Landry County Sheriff's Office. We're just trying to get the word out about the important needed repairs of our senior center. We'd appreciate it if you'd consider coming."

Mrs. Cates literally fans herself at the end of his little speech. It makes me want to punch her in the face, which would be very wrong since she's pushing eighty-five. Also, I know how she feels. Ripped, gravelly voice, sultry eyes. He's the whole package. Jerk.

"And moving on," I say after she closes the door. We walk to the sidewalk and continue toward the next house. "So, I get why you thought it would be amusing to punish me by making me hand out all these flyers, but there's one thing I don't understand."

"What's that?"

"Why are you here?" He knocks on the next door. We go through our entire spill and are heading to the next house when he answers.

"I need to learn the community, and I thought this would be a good way to start. I can also guarantee that you stay out of trouble for at least one night." He smiles at me. Damn. That thing must have taken years of braces to achieve because I refuse to believe he was simply born with perfect teeth. "It's the same reason you're taking me to this pancake thing."

"Excuse me?"

"You're taking me to this fundraiser, sticking by my side while you introduce me around, and then I'm returning you home," he says. "No witty haikus about anyone's ass are going up on my watch."

"That wasn't part of the deal. You said I just had to deliver flyers," I argue. I don't mind showing up at a community event with the man the entire single female (and at least one guy) population wants, but I can't let him get away with dictating what I do. Or putting a cramp in my fun.

"And you're paying," he adds.

"Why don't I just give you a blow job to top it all off?"

"Don't tempt me," he growls back.

We're in the middle of a stare-down when Mr. Robbins opens his door. We spin to greet him. He listens to what we have to say, shakes Owen's hand, and winks at me as he closes the door.

I stomp down the porch steps to the next door with Owen close on my heels. I don't wait for him to knock this time; I just throw open the door and walk inside.

"Wait," he calls. A strong arm wraps around my waist. I'm pulled against his warm chest as he tries to pull me back outside. "What are you doing?" he whispers.

"What are you doing?" Dad asks, stepping out of his home office.

"Oh, perfect timing," Austen adds, following Dad out. I feel Owen tense behind me as he tries to put the pieces together. "And you brought a guest."

"The food is ready," Mom announces from the other end of the house. "What are y'all waiting for? Oh, I'll set another place."

"No, that's—" Owen stammers. He still has a firm grip on my waist. I'm not complaining. Reed appears from Dad's office and smacks Owen on the chest.

"You should give in. It's easier that way," he says on the way down the hall.

"Come on, it's family dinner night." I sadly pull his arm from around my body. Taking his hand, I pull him down the hall behind me.

Rand and Brontë greet us in the dining room. Mom has one of her famous King Ranch casseroles on the table. There are also homemade tortilla chips, ranch-style beans, roasted broccoli, and dilled cucumber salad. My stomach growls just looking at it.

"Is there somewhere I can wash up?" he asks. That's a good choice. He's shaken a lot of hands in the last hour and a half. I point him to the bathroom and head back to the dining room.

"What is this about?" Austen asks when I return.

"He's making me distribute flyers for the pancake dinner door-to-door."

"Because of the bulletin board?"

"Yeah. I thought I'd get back by ambushing him with family dinner night." Seems perfectly fitting to me. That whole eye for an eye thing.

"Makes sense." Reed shrugs. I knew there was a reason we were best friends in high school. Mom smacks him playfully on the arm.

"We're not punishment," she admonishes.

"Well, of course, it goes without saying that you're not, but your daughters..." I would argue, but the sound of the bathroom door distracts me. Owen, sans sexy cowboy hat, slides into the seat next to mine. Since when has our bathroom soap smelled so good? I lean over for another whiff. That can't be our soap.

"Stop smelling me," he mutters. "Thank you for letting me crash dinner. Had I been warned, I would have picked up something. I apologize for the intrusion."

"Don't be ridiculous," Mom gushes. "You are welcome to dinner anytime. Any friend of Eliot's is."

"We're not friends," I blurt out right as Owen chimes in with, "Closer to parole officer."

"Did you just say you're like my parole officer?" I ask.

"I did," he answers.

"Then I'm not taking you to the pancake dinner. No parolee would take their PO to dinner." My family looks at me like I'm insane.

"Yes, you are." His eyes narrow at me. I meet his glare with one of my own. "And you'll enjoy it."

"Make. Me." We're officially in a stare-off.

"I can, but you won't sit for a week," he snarls back.

"Quick, someone get a bucket of ice water before clothes start coming off," Reed says. A blush races up Owen's face. I'm sure it's a match to the one on mine. I guess we both forgot where we were for a minute.

"Okay, let's just pass the food and try to pick something else to talk about. Like the weather," Mom says.

Everyone laughs as the noise of dishes being passed drowns out my embarrassment. Conversation amps up as we both turn back to the table. Dad asks Owen about something involving the county which gives me a chance to take a quick glance at him. His color seems to have returned to normal. There's a sharp kick to my shin.

"What?" I mouth at Brontë. She just grins at me, cutting her eyes between us. "Shut up," I mouth.

Sisters. I love them. They're great. Sisterhood and all that shit. Blah, blah, blah. I'm thinking of axe-murdering the youngest one. Possibly the other one just for good measure. It would be easier than continuing to explain to them that nothing is going to happen between the hotter-than-Hades deputy and plain, old me.

OWEN

That conniving vixen ambushed me. I don't really mind. It's been a long time since I've had a home cooked meal. Elise is no slouch in the kitchen. I liked both of her parents, even if I did manage to embarrass myself in front of them. At least the term "blow job" wasn't thrown out this time. No reason to introduce her dad to the hard-on I get every time his daughter opens her mouth.

The next night, I have to work, so I can't help with the remaining flyers. I see Eliot around town though while I'm on patrol. My sightings are usually acknowledged with a middle finger. That woman really does need to be laid over my legs for a good spanking. No, don't picture that or I'll never get my jeans on.

Tonight is finally the night of the pancake dinner, except around here it's called supper. Either way, I'm having an anxiety attack as I dig through my closet. As soon as I got off work, I rushed home. I've showered, shaved, and deodorized. My hair is neatly combed. I've slapped on aftershave I think she'll like. Now if I can just find a shirt.

I'm looking for pretty much anything in my closet that's not khaki. Don't get me wrong; I love being a sheriff's deputy. The only thing that varies from winter to summer is the cowboy hat I was unofficially told to get. The chief said it sets us apart in the community. How, when you live in a town full of cowboy hats? I don't question it; I just wear the hat.

Not tonight though. I don't know about Eliot, but this is as close to a date as I've gotten with her. It's important I look good. I pull a blue paisley button-down out of the back of the closet. It still has the tags on it from Christmas. My mom thought I needed a new wardrobe to blend in better with the locals. Whatever. It'll work.

I bought a new pair of dark jeans for tonight. My ass has a poetic standard to live up to now. Besides, Eliot staring at my ass isn't all bad.

I have just enough time to check myself in the mirror before I need to leave for Eliot's house. Not too bad. I offered to drive us, but she suggested we walk. I guess they're expecting a record crowd and parking is at a premium.

Turns out, she lives only two blocks from me. I'm knocking on her door before I know it. I take a steadying breath right before the door swings open. It's knocked right out of my lungs at the sight of her. She's stunning. Her hair is long and curled with just the front pulled back in a clip. She's in a dress that skims her thighs right above her knees. I'm rendered speechless.

"I like your shirt," she says.

"Yeah?" I sound like an idiot.

"Yeah, it's nice."

"Thanks. You look nice too." And I just proved I *am* an idiot. "I mean, you look amazing. Are you ready?"

"Almost. Come in while I finish."

"I can't imagine how you could need any more." She rewards me with a smile. She turns and I follow her inside.

"I'll just be a second," she says as she heads down a hallway. I take a good look around her small home. It's tidy just like I would expect it to be. I imagine everything I don't see behind the cabinet doors is perfectly organized. Eliot wouldn't put up with anything less. I make a mental note to do a better job in my own home.

"Do you cook?" I ask. Based on the line of canisters on her kitchen counter, I would guess so.

"Only if I want to eat," she answers, walking back into the room. She's pulled on a pair of boots. Shame to hide all that glorious leg.

"Always a smartass."

"Each and every time. Wouldn't you be sad if I changed?"

"Absolutely." I know she was asking a rhetorical question, but I had to answer. I like Eliot feisty and smart-mouthed. I know I give her a lot of grief for being the local law enforcement terror, but I like how complicated she is. Secretly. There's no reason she needs to know that.

"So what trouble have you gotten into since I last saw you?" I tease.

"I have been perfectly angelic." She picks up her purse.

"Why do I have a hard time believing that?" I follow her out her front door. We stop while she locks up.

"You just don't know an angel when you see one." I meet her golden eyes. She smirks.

"Don't be so sure." I know she's joking, but I'm not. She takes my arm as we walk down the sidewalk toward the American Legion Hall where the pancakes await. There's a small smile on her lips. One I think I put there. Suddenly, I feel ten feet tall.

seven

OWEN

"THIS IS, without a doubt, the best thing ever created in the history of the world," I tell Eliot between bites. Not only is it a dinner of pancakes, it's an all-you-can-eat one. Why don't more communities have fundraisers involving breakfast food? It's a game changer.

"That might be a little overdramatic," she answers. She hasn't done much more than pick at her pancakes. I'm currently on my second helping.

"I don't think so. No." I stab a bite of sausage and stuff it in my mouth. Did I mention breakfast meat is included?

"I thought you were here to meet the public," she smirks.

"You can stand a few more minutes eating pancakes with me." She rolls her eyes. "Fine," I say finally, pushing back my empty plate. "Let's do this." I stand, take our plates, and walk them to the trash. Eliot trails behind me. When I turn around, I almost run into her. "Jesus, woman."

"I like to think so." I laugh. She's so damn quick-witted. It's one of the many things I like about her.

"So, what's the plan?" I ask.

"We're going to work around the outside. That's where most of the people here to visit will be located," she says. "We'll swing by the silent auction. You'll bid on something that shows you're a part of the community but not on the take."

"On the take?" She gives me a side-eye, so I nod in agreement.

"Then we can get dessert and focus on the middle of the room."

"Wait, there's dessert?"

"Come on," she says, wrapping her arm in mine. "Be a good boy, and you can have dessert later." Now, say that while I have you pressed against the wall. Focus.

We head over to the drink table. She introduces me to several men lingering close by. We visit for a few minutes before moving on.

It takes us close to twenty minutes to find our way to the silent auction. Slowly, we move down the long set of tables looking at everything up for offer. There are the usual gift cards, baskets full of stuff, and local hunting trips.

But what catches my eye is a two-night stay at an upscale condo on Lake Austin. My brain heats at the idea of Eliot barely covered and basking in an infinity pool overlooking the lake. We could find something to eat, maybe check out the live music on Sixth Street first. It sounds like the perfect date night.

Now I just need to convince the perfect date. The one currently considering bidding on a Henry Lever Action Model X .45-70 hunting rifle. Fuck, she's sexy.

Damn, it seems like I'm not the only one interested in

the condo. The bid is already over two grand. That's a lot on a deputy's salary. Maybe the pie for a month is more my speed. It guarantees twelve pies whenever I want them. That and the bid is only at a hundred. Hmm, what else? Don't need the six free babysitting nights.

"Did you donate anything, Eliot?"

"I always donate free accounting services," she answers. Shit. I don't think I need help balancing my checkbook.

"What would you suggest I bid on?"

"Let's see." She moves back down the table, pulling me with her. "I saw you lusting after the pies so slap one-fifty down on those. You may not win; she makes damn good pies. They're a popular item every year." She moves farther along. "Do you like to bar-b-que?"

"Not really. I don't cook much."

"So no to anything cooking-wise." She studies the items in front of us. "Hunt?" I shake my head. "Fish?" No to that one too. "Do not bid on my brother-in-law's condo. That thing is going to go for way too much," she mumbles, moving along. "Oh, here we go. You're into reading, right?"

"Who isn't into reading?" Seems like a rhetorical question to me. She rolls her eyes again and points to a set of mint-condition county history books. I quickly scrawl my name on the sheet with a price I can afford.

"Let's see. One more should do it." She peruses further down the table. "Freezer of meat?"

"No space."

"Ornamental tree?"

"No lawn."

"Ballroom dance lessons?"

"Only if you'll take them with me."

She takes the pen, signs my name, and puts an amount.

"Done," she says with a flourish. Is she really going to take dance lessons with me?

"What did you bid on? The rifle?" I ask.

"Of course. And the personal catfish fry. And the Jeep tour of the bluebonnets when they're blooming again." She's better at this than I am. "Come on, we have more schmoozing to do. At this rate, you should be in the perfect position to run for sheriff when Sheriff Rogers retires. Shouldn't be too long now."

I'm still contemplating her suggestion I run for sheriff when Reed walks up with a group of men following. I feel like this describes his personality exactly. He's one of those guys that everyone wants to hang out with in the hope that some of his charm rubs off. He slaps me on the back when we meet.

"I see you're a glutton for punishment," he says with a nod at Eliot. I open my mouth to defend her, but she's too quick.

"Bite me, Reed," she fires back. I should know by now that she can defend herself.

"Oh sweetie, I have a feeling we'd both be in trouble for that." He throws a lazy arm over her shoulder and squeezes her against him.

I've got to admit I'm jealous. It was explained to me at the family dinner that they were best friends in high school. That there has never been anything between them. But that doesn't quell the need to glare at him. He winks back at me. That doesn't help.

"Speaking of," he continues as if I'm not trying to drill a hole in the back of his head with my scowl. "What are you doing Thursday night?"

Eliot's eyes cut to mine for just a second before focusing on the floor. "I'm busy," she says vaguely. My focus shifts to her. What is she planning for a quiet Thursday night? I just hope it's a misdemeanor and not a felony.

"Come on, Eliot," Reed whines. "We need a catcher. Rafe's decided he has to celebrate his anniversary instead of playing on Thursday." He grins at a man I assume is Rafe next to him. "Please," Reed begs.

"Fine," she says after the remaining men join Reed in his plea. Eliot in catcher's gear? I can tell you where I'll be Thursday night. Right behind home plate.

"Thank you, Eliot." Reed squeezes her again and smacks a kiss to the side of her head. "Hey, do you play softball?" he asks me. I shrug noncommittally. "I'll take that as a yes. Next time." He moves on to the next group of people.

"Catcher, huh?" I ask.

"In high school. Do you play?"

"I have. I was a runner in school though."

"Really?"

"Yep. I ran relays and the mile. Medaled at state, so remember that when you're scheming."

"The more you know," she smirks. "I think that earns you some peach cobbler."

"Now you're talking my love language."

ELIOT

Son of a bitch. Now I have to take dance lessons. With the guy who keeps trying to arrest me. The sexy, smoldering, stacked guy that makes my skin tingle in anticipation every time he touches me. And I'm supposed to survive being twirled around a room with his big hands on my waist.

If I had just won that stupid gun. No. I've already shot the sheriff once. No need to tempt fate a second time.

That lucky bastard won all three of the items he bid on. I got a fish fry for twenty of my closest friends.

In retrospect, I might be the luckier bastard. Dad has already volunteered to have the party in the backyard, and I get to spend six weeks with Owen's hands caressing my waist. Again. However, doing so to manhandle me out of my parents' house didn't count.

"Well, that was crazy," he says, walking back over to me from settling up. It's the first time he's left my side all evening. I'm not complaining; just feels a little odd is all. I'm used to doing everything on my own. I can't think of any event I've been escorted to by a man in this town since prom. And that was skinny Clive Bates, so I'm not sure that counts.

"Are people always this excited about winning free accounting services?" he teases when I don't answer.

"It's like winning the lottery."

"Really?"

"Yes. It's discovering tax-free buried treasure, free accounting, and then winning the lottery. In that order."

"That's how it is then?" He laughs.

"That's how it is." The room is starting to empty. All in all, it hasn't been a bad evening. "You ready to go?"

"Whenever you are." He takes my hand, and I try to fight the goosebumps as I pull him toward the door. I have got to get my shit together or the waltz will turn into the forbidden dance.

"Hey, are y'all heading out?" Reed asks, catching up to us near the door. "A couple of us were going for a beer. Thought Owen might want to come. You're off duty, right?"

"I am."

"Don't you think there's been enough excitement for the new guy for one night?" I point out. Not that I'm his babysitter, but the idea of Reed sharing every embarrassing story about me from high school is horrifying.

"And Rand has a baby." He's standing next to Reed with Keats in a sling. He's rocking back and forth patting him on the butt. Keats, not Reed.

"We're not taking the baby, Mom," Reed fires back. "Interested?" he asks Owen.

"Yeah, I'll meet you after I walk Eliot home. Which bar?"

"The Cougar Den."

"Really?"

"Yeah, I don't think they thought that name out. It sounds worse than it is," he says. "Unless you're into that." I glare at Reed.

"Sounds like the perfect end to the evening." Now I glare at Owen.

I watch them discuss their plans like I'm at a tennis tournament. My stomach feels queasy. This is happening. What little sex appeal I have is about to be wiped away by tales of barfing in the locker room and farting in class.

After several hardy handshakes, because that's what we do in this part of the world, Owen takes my hand again. I'm not sure that law enforcement should be quite this touchy-feely.

"Tonight was nice," he says when we break free of the crowd. We're slowly walking toward my house. Fall isn't quite here yet, but the temperatures are no longer unbearable. "Thank you for going with me."

"You should have held out for a better offer," I quip.

"Don't do that." He steps in front of me, spins, and stops. In my defense, it's impossible not to crash into his chest. His hand grips my chin and pulls my face up until my gaze meets his. "I scored the very best offer out there. Any man would be honored to have you on their arm. Understand?"

"Mhm," I say, nodding my head like an idiot. He steps back next to me, continuing down the sidewalk.

I, on the other hand, am a puddle of goo on the sidewalk. My ovaries are shooting off fireworks. My skin vibrates. My heart feels like that cartoon dog with his heart pounding out of his chest. Owen stops and looks at me like I'm insane. I might be.

"Are you coming?" he asks.

"Yep, yeah, absolutely." I do an awkward jog thing to catch up. We walk the rest of the block in silence. I pull my keys out of my purse when we reach my porch.

"Well, this is me. Have fun drinking. Thanks again." I push open the door, step inside, and hurriedly close it behind me. Like I'm fifteen. Jesus, what is wrong with me?

The last thing I see before it firmly closes is Owen's grin. "Thank you," he yells through the door. "I had a really good time. I'm sure I'll see you soon."

I press my back against the door and slide down in mortification. Well, that's one less guy I'll have to worry about. Between whatever mental lapse I just had and Reed's tale of the time my high school braces almost killed Brandon Cates, he'll be long gone.

eight

OWEN

FOR THE FIRST time in a long time, I feel like I might have found a home. Since the pancake sign incident and subsequent flier disbursement, people call a greeting to me when they see me around town. Sure, some of those still involve my ass, but I've heard worse in my career.

I even enjoyed attending the pancake supper. My bank account is a little lighter, but it was for a good cause. And I got to spend the entire night with Eliot. Almost. Right up until she slammed the door in my face. I like to think I was too much of a temptation for her. A man can dream, right?

I did send a small bouquet of flowers as a thank you. Not roses; that's a little too over the top. Whether she knows it or not, I'm counting that as date number one. Especially since she didn't have to beg me not to arrest her at the end of the night. I would not have been opposed to putting my handcuffs to good use though. I grin at the thought as I work on my reports at my desk.

"I don't know what's got into you, but that's quite the

naughty grin you have going," Cherylynn says on the way to the coffee pot. I pull a scowl at her, and she laughs. "I'm thinking all that good cheer somehow involves your date with Eliot Caraway. Am I right?" I notice everyone in the room has grown quiet. I'll be the center of gossip for this week too.

"It wasn't a date. I coerced her to take me," I answer loud enough for everyone to hear. Laughter fills the room. It's not like I could have forced her if she had refused, but I don't need even more speculation circulating about us.

"Owen, I went to school with Eliot. You can't coerce her to do anything she doesn't want to do." That makes me feel weirdly impressed with myself. She walks back to the front of the office.

"She's also a serious ballbuster if you piss her off," Ray mumbles. "Trust me, don't get on her bad side. She's much scarier than her sisters." That observation pisses *me* off. Dude, don't disparage the future Mrs. Steele. Oooh, I'm a riot. I'm laughing hysterically at that thought on the inside. I shoot a scowl at Ray on the outside.

I have the evening shift again. Slowly the office empties. The sun is setting when I start my patrol.

I don't mind working late actually. Especially on the weekdays. Barring a major accident on the interstate, not much happens around here after dark. The kids are in school. Their parents have work. It's pretty tame.

It's past nine when my radio crackles to life. "Hey, Owen?"

"What's up, Lara?" We're not very formal here.

"I'm getting calls about someone drag racing up River Road."

"I'll check it out."

"Thanks, Owen."

I would guess it's a couple of kids who should be home prepping for school tomorrow. I'll haul them home, explain to their parents about the dangers of racing, and be back out within the hour. Parents hate being lectured. They usually take care of the problem for me.

I swing a U-turn on Main and head toward the road that runs next to the river. It's not long before I see the problem.

A deep purple Camaro is burning all the rubber off its tires in the middle of the street. I flip on my lights and pull next to it before it can take off. I should have known it wasn't some kid. They're way more responsible than the red-headed accountant sitting in the driver's seat.

I step out of the cruiser and hike my gun belt up. I'm seriously thinking about using parts of it on her. Settling the hat firmly on my head, I stomp to the driver's door and jerk it open.

"Get. Out," I snarl. She has the audacity to look at me with big puppy dog eyes. I come within a hair's breadth of caving. "Out." She sighs. Then she slides out from behind the steering wheel. "What the fuck, Eliot?" You know I was raised better than to cuss at a woman, but this one is the most frustrating woman I've ever met.

"Whoa. Language." She smirks. I both want to throttle her and kiss the smirk off her face. I choose neither.

"Get in the cruiser." We've played this game before. She shrugs and walks to the passenger side.

It's not until I climb back inside and turn toward her that I realize her legs are bare to the middle of her thighs. She's wearing a miniskirt. Her flowy blouse is cut to accentuate her perfect cleavage. How do I do my job with her looking like temptation itself?

"Is that your car?" It comes out a little hoarse, so I clear my throat. The corner of her lips lifts slightly.

"Nope."

"Please tell me you didn't steal someone's car."

"I borrowed one from Cam. She works at the body shop. Crackerjack of a mechanic. She offered a Corvette she's working on, but I thought the '67 Camaro had a better sound. The torque on that beauty is insane too." She's just babbling on about the very thing I'm here to bust her for. And damn it, I'm listening. But I remember I owe this woman nothing. She slammed her door in my face.

"I'm writing you a ticket for reckless driving," I bark.

"I would assume. I mean, do you see those black marks?"

"You do understand I can throw you in jail for ninety days, right? You'll also face a fine."

"Yes, okay."

"They can suspend your driver's license."

"I'm not really that into driving anyway."

"You're giving me a fucking aneurysm, you know that?" I yell. She stares back at me.

"They might need to start a swear jar at the station."

"Get out, return the car, and go home," I say through gritted teeth. I know I should give her a ticket, but I don't have the mental prowess tonight to spar with Eliot Caraway.

"Thanks," she says. Then she does something that will have me in a tailspin for the rest of my shift. She leans over and presses her lips to mine. It's just for a moment and she's gone by the time I recover, but it makes getting fired for letting another misdemeanor slide so worth it.

* * *

ELIOT

Yes, you read that right. For some unexplained reason, I decided the perfect time to kiss Owen was as he was letting me off with a warning. Again. What are the charges for sexually harassing an officer of the law?

He looked like a deer in the headlights. Should I add that to the list? I'm almost positive no high school kid went around kissing the sheriff. I think I'll just chalk it up to gas fumes from revving the Camaro's engine.

"So, how did it go? Did you redline her?" Cam asks when I pull the car back into her shop.

"I didn't want to blow the engine up. Besides, I got busted before I had a chance. I did several nice donuts, and the burn marks are impressive." I give her the keys and run my hand back over the paint one more time. "Say, how much for one of these?"

"Around twenty-five grand. It's supposed to be Carter's new car. But he's a soft touch. You can probably talk him out of it for less."

"I might ask him about it the next time I'm at the bank. He can sell me the car and finance it too," I give it one last caress. "Hey, thanks for letting me borrow it."

"Anytime," she answers. I wave as she lowers the overhead door. It was fun. Way better than climbing the water tower.

But back to that kiss. In the brief time our lips touched, I could tell his were soft but firm. You know, like he's a trumpet player with a lip balm addiction.

I also think I heard a moan. I'm not sure if it was him or me. And do you know how people say their minds just go blank? Not mine. It was like a slideshow at super speed. There were phallic symbols, flowers opening, old movie kisses, trees, peach pie. You name it, it was there. I don't know if I'm hard up or hungry.

I wonder how long it'll take him to figure out I only act bad when he's on duty? I even dressed for the occasion. It wasn't lost on me how he made a full perusal of the goods either. He's beginning to make me believe that I might just have more to offer than good math skills. I shouldn't get my hopes up though. He's probably filing a complaint already.

I've marked another item off my list. The only thing left to do tonight is a mug of tea and a true crime documentary. I drive home and let myself inside. I shower the remaining fumes from my body. Sporting my favorite pajamas (the ones with sheep on them), I settle onto the couch with my mug of tea.

A fist pounds on my front door like it's trying to beat it off the hinges. Who in the hell makes a social call this late? I set my mug on the table and paddle in my fuzzy socks to the door.

Here's the thing about our small town. We all know each other, so none of us think twice about jerking the door open without checking who's outside. I should have checked. When I open it, Owen stands on the other side.

I'm still trying to figure out why he's here when his hand wraps around the back of my neck and he pulls me to him. He sighs when our lips meet like he's found where he belongs. The lingering question about who moaned earlier is answered. It's definitely me. My body relaxes against his as his tongue insists on entry into my mouth.

He growls when his tongue slides across mine. He's a growler. That's good to know. I'll add "growler" under the spreadsheet I'm thinking about starting the minute I'm free. Which, at this moment, I hope is never.

His hand wraps in my hair. He angles my head to deepen the kiss. I'm ruined. I've never been kissed this well.

Slowly, as if it pains him, he releases me. Our mouths part and I open my eyes to find his glazed with what I can only hope is lust. He removes his hands from my hair.

He takes a step back, never taking his eyes from mine. Then he takes another. Finally, his lust morphs into something tinged with anger. But not the kind of anger that's frightening, the kind that lingers when your needs aren't quite fulfilled.

"That," he starts, then stops to clear his throat. "That is how you kiss me next time you want to avoid getting a ticket. I can't fight against a kiss like that." He sounds angry as he says it, but I know better. "Understand?"

"Yes, sir," I whisper. His fists clench at his sides. His eyes close for the count of three and then open, directed right at me. Without another word, he turns back toward the cruiser idling on the curb. I watch as he stomps to it and drives away.

This time when I slide down the inside of the locked door, it's for a completely different reason. I'm in trouble here. He kisses me again like that, I won't be able to fight against him either.

Shit. I've got to tell someone about this. I need help figuring out what to do from here. I don't care what time it is, I crawl to my phone and call Austen. I don't know how many times she kept me up listening to her problems with Reed. Turnabout is fair play.

"Eliot?" she slurs. "What's wrong?"

"He kissed me." That's all I have to say for her to wake up fully. I hear Reed grumble in the background. I don't feel bad about that either. I'm the reason he passed high school Pre-cal.

"His lips on yours?" she rapid fires.

"Yes."

"Tongue?"

"Yes."

"Where were his hands?"

"My hair."

"Good. So he's still a gentleman and hasn't decided to play grabass. What did you do?" Austen asks.

"I kissed him back. I guess I'm a moaner. I never knew that."

"Is he a moaner?" I hear Reed protest in the background. Austen shushes him.

"No. He sighs and then growls."

"Okay, not bad. Are you sitting on the floor freaking out?"

"Yes." I can't lie; I am a little freaked out.

"Is this like the time Paul Rush licked you in the hallway?"

"Gross. No. I don't mind Owen's tongue making contact with my skin." I flattened Paul about two seconds after he licked me. I don't want you to think I let just anyone go around licking me.

"Then I'm going to give you the same advice a very wise woman named Eliot Caraway gave me once. Just relax and see where it goes. You can end it any time you want if you decide you want to. I like Owen. Reed likes Owen. I can think of worse things than hooking up with the new deputy," she says.

Don't you hate when someone turns your advice back on yourself? If I were there with her, I might have to smack her. And then Reed, just for good measure.

"Fine." I plop back on my couch. "I'll just roll with the punches. Whatever. You suck at advice."

72

"Why do you think Brontë and I turn to you all the time?" She laughs. "You're the wizened wizard in our group. Now go to bed. You have work in the morning."

"Okay. Good night, guys," I say.

"Good night, horndog," I hear Reed yell. Then there are some wrestling noises and giggling. I hang up in a hurry. At least one of us is getting a happy ending tonight.

nine

ELIOT

I'M OVER THE KISS. Well, not over it exactly, but I'm less undone by it. I went to the office the next day and crunched the shit out of some numbers. Nothing like a good spreadsheet to tamp down those hormonal urges. Remember, if you ever develop a crush on someone you shouldn't, run a profit and loss sheet for the local funeral home. That will sober you up in a hurry.

Tonight, I'll have my body parts all over him. Not in a good way, though. It's the first dance lesson, and I promised to go. I never back out of my promises. Even if those promises lead to disaster.

I'm positive he'll walk away with several bruised toes and possibly a talus break. That's the top bone in your foot. Yeah, I had to look it up too. I didn't want to have to ask the emergency room doctor.

I have no idea what to wear to adult dance lessons. I'm guessing a pink leotard and tutu is not it though. Shame, I think I'd look pretty badass in those.

I decided a midcalf dress and low, chunky, closed-toed heels are more appropriate. I assume we'll meet at the studio, but when I open the door to leave, Owen is standing outside with his fist up ready to knock.

"Hey," I manage.

"Hey," he answers. Good to see we're on the same page. "You look nice."

"You too." He does. He's freshly showered. He's opted for navy slacks and a subtle striped button-down. He also has on a pair of dress shoes. "Oh, am I dressed okay? You know, for dancing. Tripping the light fantastic. Grinding out the forbidden dance." Why do I keep bringing that up?

"I'm not sure about grinding, but you're perfect for ballroom," he answers with a laugh. "Did you want to drive or walk?" Everything in this town is a short walk away. If the weather is nice, I prefer to walk. It helps counterbalance sitting at a desk all day.

"Walk." I pull the door closed. "So, should we talk about that kiss?" I ask as we start for the dance studio.

"Why? I wanted to kiss you so I did. If you don't like it, let me know. Otherwise, I think people talk things out too much. I think it's good sometimes to just go with your instinct and let the chips fall where they may. Did you enjoy it?" He looks down at me. I can feel a blush creeping up my face. Did I like it? Are The Dallas Cowboys America's team? Freaking yes.

"I did," I say instead.

"Then we've talked it out." He nods and continues down the sidewalk. What's scary is I completely agree with him. I'm not a person who thinks everything needs to be hyper-analyzed to death. "I'll probably do it again too." I grin stupidly as we turn the corner.

"Good to know. Thanks for the warning."

"Like it says, I'm here to serve and protect." He smiles at me. "Is there any other way I can serve you?"

I giggle. Like a schoolgirl. I'm throwing a disclaimer out here. I do not giggle. I didn't when I was a girl; I don't do it now. Except when gorgeous men offer their services, I guess. I keep giggling until Owen laughs.

"Too much?" he asks, and I start to laugh all over again.

We reach the dance studio still chuckling. Inside, there are at least a dozen couples signed up for the adult ballroom class, including both of my sisters and their significant others. Owen shakes hands with Reed, Rand, and most of the other men. They all look a little uncomfortable. There are a lot of excited women standing in a group though.

"Eliot." They greet me like I'm Norm entering *Cheers*.

"Everyone."

"You know half the town is jealous of all the attention you're getting from the new meat in town," Hailey says in a conspiratorial whisper.

I'm not worried about her. She married Chad Weston. I once nut-punched Chad for making moves on my sister. He's kept his distance ever since. I was glad to see they had two kids though. It's good to know I didn't do too much damage to those gonads.

"I'm sure he'd tell a different story," I respond. "And we should probably choose a different word than meat."

"Oh, I don't know. He keeps looking over at you," Tina adds. "Also, you started the use of meat to describe guys." She doesn't worry me either. Her husband is the smoking-hot attorney in town. And at no time have I assaulted his man parts. Just to be clear.

I start to protest. Before I can, Mrs. Bradford sweeps into the room. She claps her hands, and we hurry to find our partner. She's the same dance teacher I had when I was still rocking the tutu. Owen moves to stand next to me as she doles out instructions.

"Gentlemen, you'll take your partner thusly," she says. I'm going to have to start using the word "thusly" more. It's a good one.

Before she finishes her demonstration on Reed, Owen takes my hand and pulls me snugly against him. One hand cradles mine perfectly; the other slides to my back bracing me expertly. Hmm, something tells me he's not telling me everything.

"We're going to start with a simple one-two step." Poor Reed is stuck as her partner again. "One-two, one-two." Owen moves me forward a few steps before he swirls me around the dance floor keeping perfect rhythm to the music Mrs. Bradford started.

"Dude, what the hell?" Reed yells. "Mrs. Bradford, Owen is a ringer."

"Sorry," he says, stopping us in the middle of the dance floor. He shrugs. "My mom owns a dance studio. I've been dancing since I was small. I've got a couple of trophies back home to prove it."

My jaw hits the floor. What? What? No wonder his ass has a six-pack. He has a dancer's ass. Well, great. Now I want to touch it. The last thing I need is one more thing to focus on. Jeez.

"Wonderful. You can help me with the class," Mrs. Bradford informs him. So much for my professional dance partner. Now I have to share him with the whole class.

"I appreciate that, ma'am. But I'm just here to dance with Eliot," he answers.

WHAT? The room of women, and several of the men,

swoon in unison. My mind fills with that emoji of the yellow guy with a bomb coming from his head.

"Very well," she says and starts the music again. Owen pulls me back into his arms. We start around the room again.

"What are you doing?" I ask. "Why did you bid on the dance lessons if you can already dance?"

"Because I wanted to dance with you. Remember, you said if I bought them, you would accompany me all six weeks."

"I know, but you don't want to dance with me. I'm horrible at it. I have two left feet. You're going to get hurt."

"You don't have two left feet. And if I can't lead you around this dance floor, well then Mom should strip me of my thirteen and under Illinois all-state ballroom championship." My jaw drops to the floor again.

"Oh my god. You're not just good, you're a champion?" I shriek.

"Are you impressed?"

"I'm rendered speechless, and that's not easy to do."

"Good. That's what I was aiming for." Before I can analyze that to death, Mrs. Bradford stops the music.

"Excuse me, Mr...." She points at Owen.

"Steele or just Owen," he answers.

"Please come demonstrate how to lead. This is like being at a junior high dance." Did I mention my dance teacher is also a ballbuster? That must be why I've always liked her.

"Okay. Guys, you can't lead properly if you dance out here." He pushes me to arm length. "Don't watch your feet. Remember, dance tells a story. Frame your partner between your arms." He pulls me to him suddenly, and I gasp. I can't help it.

"She needs to be flush against you unless you're doing something like the Viennese waltz. If it's Latin, your leg is between hers like she's grinding on it." He pushes his thigh against my nether regions. Great, now I get to dance in wet panties.

"For a simple two-step, she wants us in a simple closed position. Four points of contact." He counts them out as he demonstrates, using me as his muse. "Don't forget, you want to be near her, and there's no principal here to tell you otherwise." Everyone laughs.

Mrs. Bradford starts the music again and moves around the room correcting students. She never even approaches us.

"You're amazing," I tell Owen.

He smiles. If this was all to impress me, he's succeeded. "Why did your mother think you needed to learn to dance so well?"

"To impress the right woman," he answers. My face burns again at the compliment. Damn, he's on his game tonight.

"And what did your dad say about it?"

"It'll help get me laid." I laugh. "He's a cop, but he supported whatever decision my mother made. Still does. He's wrapped around her finger."

"Really?"

"Yep. He's a burly desk sergeant in Chicago, but he's completely gone for my mom."

"A real cinnamon roll then," I observe. I like his parents already.

"Yeah. I guess so. It works for them, so whatever."

"They sound amazing."

"They are," he agrees, smiling at me. "Now, woman, let's step this up a little."

I squeal when he spins me out, then dips me when I return. The others stop dancing to applaud. I rarely want the attention of the class on me, but this time, it feels nice. For the first time, it feels like turning thirty isn't the end of the world.

* * *

OWEN

Am I the nerd who had to learn how to dance like a pro growing up? Yes. Was Mom right when she said it would impress the right woman? Absolutely.

As much whining as I used to do when I was marched off to dance class, I regret none of it now. I'll wait until later to drop the bomb that I also learned how to box. I have to space my ammunition out. There's only so much I can impress her with.

"Oh my gosh," Eliot says as she unlocks her front door. This time, instead of slamming it in my face, she leaves it open for me to follow her inside. "I never knew how hard ballroom dancing is. I'm starving." I close the door and follow her into her kitchen. "Make yourself comfortable while I throw us together a snack," she says, pointing to her couch.

I wander over to her bookshelf instead. You know I can't pass up a library no matter what size. Bookstores are my kryptonite. The bottom shelf is all accounting books, but there are two shelves of fiction and one of history.

Her taste is as eclectic as she is. I'm thumbing through a well-worn copy of *John Carter of Mars* when I hear her set something on the coffee table behind me.

"You just 'threw together' a charcuterie board?" I ask when I turn around. "Is that smoked salmon?" She shrugs like she's embarrassed. "My god, is there anything you can't do?"

"I can't dance." She laughs. "Not like you anyway." She motions me over. I find my place on the couch. She hands me a plate, which I fill with a ridiculously diverse number of snacks. How does she find half of this around here?

"This is amazing," I add, taking a bite. She smiles her thousand-watt smile. The one that only comes out when she's truly happy. It's rare and precious because of that.

"Oh," she says, jumping back up. "Would you like a beer?"

"Sure." She hurries to the kitchen and returns with a beer I've never heard of.

"It's from one of the area microbreweries. It's really good. If you don't like it though, I have others."

I take a swig. It's possibly one of the best I've had. What rock have I been living under not to know about this place?

"This is excellent." She smiles and relaxes slightly. If I didn't know better, I'd say she's nervous. Never did I think I'd see Eliot Caraway nervous. Is it me? "Are you okay?"

"Yeah. I'm great." No, I don't think she is.

I finish my plate and stand. "Well, I should go. I have work tomorrow, as do you." I walk to the door. She follows me. "Tonight was fun."

"It was. I wonder what we'll tackle next week?"

"Maybe that grinding you're so fond of."

She grows red again.

"Thanks for the dance." I bend down and kiss her softly on the lips. I don't want her any more wary of inviting me inside than she already is. I can pull out the manners.

"It was good," she says when I pull back.

"The dance or the kiss?" I tease.

"Both?" I laugh, and she closes the door in my face again. Doesn't matter this time. Date number two was perfect.

ten

ELIOT

IF HE THINKS I'm going to be subdued by sexy good looks and charm out the wazoo, well, he's almost right. But I have a list to complete. And no amount of being waltzed around a dance floor or goodnight kisses is going to distract me.

That's why I'm sitting alone at the bar on a Friday night manifesting Harmony Ellis.

Who is Harmony Ellis you might ask? Word has it that Harmony launched her music career by getting drunk in high school at one of the parties and busting out an award-winning performance of Kelly Clarkson singing the national anthem while standing on a picnic table. Someone recorded it and sent it to one of those talent shows. The rest, as they say, is history. Or that's what I think happened. I wasn't there; I was never there.

Anyway, it became a thing of legend. Kids have been trying to emulate it ever since. I know I'm no Harmony, or Kelly either, for that matter. But I still put it on the list.

Therefore, I'm sitting at the bar waiting for the bartender to bring my drink. This is going to take a lot of alcohol if I'm dancing and singing on one of these tables.

You'll be happy to know I did not drive to this event. I have a rule about never driving drunk. I don't want my sisters to talk me out of this, so I had to walk. It's why I'm sitting in the very bar I shot fireworks in front of. A shot of tequila is set in front of me.

"Hey, Eliot."

"Hey, Kev." The bartender, Kevin, graduated the year after me. We were friendly in the hallways, and I see him enough around town to say hello, but we've never been close. Just different social groups, I guess. He was probably there to see Harmony's breakthrough moment.

"What's brought you out tonight?" he asks. What? A girl can't just drink on her own for no reason?

"Just hanging," I say.

"Anybody else coming, or are you just going it solo?"

"Solo."

"Huh. I thought you were hooking up with the new guy at the sheriff's office."

"Walk away, Kevin," I answer, making a swooshing sign with my hand. He grins, but he's smart enough to head to the other end of the bar.

He's left a lime wedge and salt. Here goes nothing. I lick the back of my hand, sprinkle some salt, lick it off, toss back the tequila, and suck on the lime. And I bet you didn't think I could party. I can party.

"You're not supposed to grimace," Kevin says as he sets down the next shot.

"Kevin," I warn. He scurries back to the other end with an even bigger grin. Stupid Kevin. I repeat the salt, lime, tequila thing again. It goes down a little easier this time.

"Are you trying to get drunk?" he asks as he sets round number three on the bar.

"Liquid courage." I can feel the tequila buzzing through my bloodstream.

By round five, Kevin doesn't seem so bad anymore. I'm not sure why we never hooked up. He's totally doable. At this point, everyone in here is totally doable. Even old man Costello, and he's my grandpa's age.

"I'm going to have to cut you off," Kevin says as he watches me slurp the lime. Jerk. It's fine. I think I'm almost ready anyway.

I weave over to the jukebox. I love a bar that still insists on keeping a jukebox instead of going digital. There's a button that flips through the songs. For some crazy reason, it takes several tries before my finger makes contact.

"What song are you looking for, darling?" some burly guy asks. Wait, I know him. He works at the feed store, I think. "How about this one?" He punches some buttons, and the perfect song comes on.

I join Shelly West belting out "Jose Cuervo." Now, I just have to figure out how to get on one of these tables. Fortunately, the burly feed guy helps me up.

I've got to tell you; I nail Shelly West. The song, not the woman. I never knew I could sing this amazing. When the song ends, another one comes on. This time, several of the other patrons join in when Toby asks "How Do You Like Me Now?" It seems like everyone likes me just fine now.

This is an amazingly free feeling. I've transitioned to beer between songs. There's a whole group of men standing around the table I'm on cheering for me. And every time I get too close to the edge several hands steady me by holding my thighs. They're so nice. I might do this every night.

"Hey, Eliot. You might want to come down from there," Kevin yells over the song. I swat at him. He's just jealous he doesn't have the chops I do for singing.

"Eliot," he yells louder. I shush him. He's interrupting my duet with LeAnn Rimes. There's a chance they need to update their jukebox. Doesn't matter. I'm still rocking this place.

"Here you go, sweetheart. You'd better wet those vocal cords." Burly feed guy hands a beer up to me. I throw it back in several hard swallows. Everyone goes wild for some reason. They get even more excited by the manly belch I let out. I should probably stagger to the restroom, but that seems hard.

"Eliot, how about something to eat?" Kevin tries.

"She's fine. Leave her alone," someone answers. My buddy, Garth, comes on this time. Everyone sings along. It's like one, big Karaoke night. Someone begins banging the tabletop in time to the music.

We're really getting going when the banging stops suddenly. It feels like all of the oxygen is sucked out of the room, and all I can think to do is keep singing.

The song ends, and the room grows silent. Everyone parts like a wave as boots stomp toward me. If they'd just choose another song, everything will be okay. I take a step off the table toward the jukebox.

Suddenly, I'm upside down, staring at the firmest ass I've ever seen. Well, if this is how I die, so be it. At least I get to see something nice before I go.

* * *

OWEN

It's a typical weekend night. I've pulled a couple of teenagers off the water tower. I'm not sure why they can't put a lock on the gate to keep people out.

I responded to a false burglar alarm at the hardware store. There was a moment when I thought something exciting was going to happen, but it turns out the owners forgot to take the cat home with them this time. They apologized profusely for the mistake.

I chased down a couple of kids on dirt bikes riding along the river to tell them they needed to find helmets. They agreed, then I'm sure went right back to jumping mounds of dirt without them. At least I tried.

Then I got the call. Not from dispatch this time. It came from the bartender at Garza's. It was the end of my shift, so I drove there immediately. I'm not prepared for what I find.

Standing on one of the tables in the center of the room, belting out a song that sounds like two cats fighting in an alley, is Eliot. That part I can handle. The fact she's in a short skirt and some guy has his hand on her thigh has me seeing red. Kevin rushes over to me. It's obvious he's lost control of the bar.

"Thank Christ, you're here," he yells over the noise. "I've tried several times to get her down, but she refuses. And she's scary." I glare at him. He heads back behind the bar.

I guess I'm expected to deal with this now that I'm here. The room goes quiet when I head for her table. She's still singing if that's what you can call it, but everyone else starts shuffling away. The hand disappears from her thigh.

The music stops, and Eliot looks around like she's waiting for the next one to start. She sways slightly as she stands in her cowboy boots on the table. Suddenly she steps toward the jukebox. She doesn't even try for the chair that's near her. Years of track payoff as I quickly move to catch her. I wrap my arms around her legs and lay her over my shoulder.

"What in the hell was going on here?" I ask the mostly male crowd. They find anywhere to look but at me. I finally give up and head for the door. With any luck, I can get her home before she starts throwing up.

But where do I take her? I doubt her family knows anything about this since they haven't been in on any of her other stunts. Shit, where are her keys?

"Owen," Kevin calls. He's waving her purse over his head from the door. "Thought you might need this." He hands it to me.

I'll be back around to deal with him later. Right now, I'm more concerned about Eliot moaning while draped over my shoulder. I motion for Kevin to open my passenger door. When I'm done easing her inside and hooking her seatbelt, he's nowhere in sight. I have no doubt if he leaves the rest of the crowd alone for too long, he'll never regain control.

I grab her purse from where Kevin left it on the hood and climb into the driver's seat. Eliot's head is propped against the headrest. She doesn't look good.

"Eliot," I say with a small shake. "Do I need to drive you to the hospital? How much did you drink?"

"Stop being a dick, Kevin," she moans. So still mostly coherent. Making what will probably be a bad decision, I drive to my apartment. Eliot is passed out or asleep by the time I get there. I'm hoping asleep. She moans when I pry her from the cruiser, but she's aware enough to sing a few more lines of something I can't identify.

"Come on, sunshine. Let's get you near a trash can." We

make it up the stairs to my door when she barfs all over both of us. It's going to be a long night, but I guess I can spend it trying to get vomit out of my gun belt.

"I don't feel good," Eliot moans.

I manage to steer her inside.

"No shit. Here." I grab a trash can right before more alcohol leaves her system the hard way. I manage to keep her hair out of it at least.

She finally finishes, and I ease her to the bathroom. Carefully slipping her blouse off, I slide one of my T-shirts on. I'm impressed I managed to do it without gagging. She shoves her skirt down while I'm trying to pull the boots off. It would be sexy if she didn't smell like a garbage can behind a bar.

I steer her toward the bed where she collapses in dramatic fashion. "I'm putting a trash can next to the bed. I don't envy you the headache you're going to have. I hope it was worth it." With the trash can next to her, the covers pulled to her chin, and some impressive snoring starting, I creep out of the room.

You're probably thinking my bringing Eliot here instead of her house is a creeper move. It's just a matter of semantics. I don't want her to be alone until I'm positive she's okay.

So I had three choices. I could take her to one of her family members, but it's late, and there's no reason to upset them. I could have taken her to her home, but I had no way to secure my gun or any clothes to change into. So, the logical thing was to bring her here. Where she's snoring in my bed. Wearing my clothes. Okay, I can see the issue now.

If I promise I'll sleep on the couch, does it sound better? Anyway, I grab some sweats and a T-shirt and head for the shower. Most of the vomit missed my gun, so it's safely locked in the safe. I'll clean the rest when I get out. I can also throw our vomit-covered clothes in the washing machine. See, nothing pervy is happening here.

So why does the very thought of her curled up in my bed make me hard enough to drive nails? Nothing a shower can't fix.

I almost had a heart attack when I walked into the bar tonight. Not because she was singing on the table. But at the thought of what could have happened to her. It makes me think I need to get to the bottom of this. I tried once before, and she shut me down. This time, she's not leaving until I find out what's going on.

eleven

ELIOT

I MIGHT HAVE DIED. That's what the searing pain in my head is telling me anyway. I can tell I'm not in my bedroom by the smell. It's not bad. It smells like bacon cooking. My eyelids open, and I realize instantly that's a mistake. This bedroom must be located on the sun.

"Uhhhhh," I moan.

"So you are alive." I recognize that sexy voice. Moaning again, I roll away from it. Why would he be here, wherever here is? "Come eat some breakfast so you can take something for your head."

Owen eases the blankets back and swings my legs around. Taking my hands, he sits me up on the edge of the bed.

"I'm fine," I say, making a feeble attempt to bat him away. My eyes refuse to open again. It's fine; I don't need to see. I can pull blind accountant off.

"Mmm." He sounds skeptical. Pfft.

"I promise you I am no stranger to the morning-after

hangover," I lie. I can count on one hand how many hangovers I've had. All of them but one took place at college. They were all equally horrible.

"Sure." I don't think he's buying it. He wraps his hand around my upper arm and pulls me to my feet.

My head pounds; my stomach roils. I'm pretty sure I'm swaying. His hand moves to my waist to steady me. I can almost hear the smirk on his face. I say hear because my eyes are simply refusing to cooperate.

"Let's get something in your stomach. That should help."

I let him guide me to the kitchen bar. He helps steady me on the stool and moves around to the kitchen side. Finally, I manage to crack my eyes open a smidge. It gives me a chance to check out the rest of his apartment.

It's a simple one-bedroom garage apartment. I would expect it to look like every bachelor pad I've ever imagined, but it doesn't.

For one, instead of a giant television, Owen has a wall of bookshelves. They are full of books. The television is a moderate one on a different wall. There's not even a calendar of naked women hanging on the fridge. No painting of dogs playing poker. I don't know, I'm just guessing here.

"So, books, huh?" I say.

"So, yes, books." And y'all thought I'm the smartass. "Eat," he demands, sliding a plate in front of me. It's filled with pancakes, fried eggs, bacon, and sausage. It makes me gag. "Trust me, the grease and carbs will help."

"I can't eat all of this," I whine.

"Eat as much as you can."

"So many calories," I mumble. He scowls at me. Yeah, I

don't even like post-drunk, morning after me. She's a little too whiny.

I look down and start mashing up my eggs. Wrapping a couple pieces of bacon in a pancake, I scoop egg onto my fork. I realize I'm hungrier than I thought when I pop it in my mouth. I close my eyes and enjoy the simple act of chewing something so good.

"Get in my mouth, daddy," I say after swallowing. It's really very good.

"Jesus," I hear Owen groan. He's staring at me when I open my eyes.

"Sorry, does dirty talking to my food make you uncomfortable?" He just shakes his head and returns to eating. I scoop up more eggs. "I have a question. How did you know where to find me?"

"The bartender called when the room started to get out of control."

"Damn, Kevin." I thump the counter with my fist for emphasis. The act causes waves of pain to shoot up my arm directly into my pounding headache. "Uhhh," I groan.

"I'm not sure Kevin should be blamed for your dancing on the table."

"I was singing," I point out. "I'll leave the dancing to you."

He rolls his eyes. "Is that what that screeching is called?"

"Keep it up, Steele, and you'll be in the same hot water as Kevin." Finally, he breaks into a smile. "So, why am I here instead of the drunk tank?"

"Because I want to know what the hell is going on with you. You could have been seriously injured last night. Or worse."

"I seem to remember you throwing me over your

shoulder like a sack of potatoes. I could have been injured then. Did everyone get a good look at my lady jewels?"

"Lady jewels?"

"Bajingo."

"What?" His eyebrows crinkle as he stares at me like I've sprouted two heads.

"Do I need to draw you a picture?" The crease between his eyebrows grows.

I bet you think I've lost my mind. It's all a part of the plan. I know he wants to know about my list. My goal is to keep him so off-balanced that he forgets all about it.

"I'm taking a shower." He's still staring at me as I climb off the stool and head for his bathroom.

Is it possible to stay in the shower long enough for him to go away? I guess we'll find out. I strip out of my clothes and turn the water as hot as I can stand it. Stepping in, I moan at how good the water feels when it hits my shoulders. Before it can get wet, I pile my hair on top of my head and wrap my hair tie around it.

Now, let's see what Officer Steele likes to use when he showers. I find the bottle of shampoo. Opening the lid, I take a deep inhale. It smells just like him. Woodsy, a little spicy. I put it back and pick up the soap gel bottle. Squeezing some into my hand, I rub it over my body. If I keep my eyes closed, I can imagine it's his hands running all over my body.

My fingers find their way between my legs. Do I dare? What if Owen catches me? Those thoughts fly from my mind when my fingers begin making slow, teasing circles on my clit. Heat rushes through my body in anticipation.

With my eyes squeezed tight, I can imagine Owen stepping inside the bathroom. He opens the shower door and steps inside. His voice would be rough when he admonishes me for starting without him.

He presses me against the shower wall with his body, his hand snaking around until he finds my clit. Does he torture me by making me wait or move quickly to make me scream in climax?

"Owen," I moan as my body tightens. "Yes," I hiss as waves of ecstasy crash over me.

Slowly, the room comes back into focus. Hot water streams over my sensitive nipples. I must be losing my mind. What possessed me to wack off in the shower of the deputy who brought me home drunk? That sounds like the start of a bad porn movie.

I turn off the water. Finding a towel, I wrap it around my body and step outside the bathroom. Owen stops short in the living room. He's holding my clothes from last night, neatly folded. I make sure the towel is secure and step toward him. His gaze lingers on the towel just a moment too long before jetting back up to my face. His cheeks turn a slight shade of pink.

"They're clean. I washed them last night," he says, holding them out. I take my time walking over. Do I still have him off-kilter? Based on the impressive bulge in his jeans, I'd say he is. Perfect.

"Do you mind if I find another pair of your sweats? I don't want to have to put back on last night's panties and in that skirt, nothing will be left to the imagination."

"Yeah, whatever you need."

Quickly, I disappear back into his bedroom. I pull the first T-shirt I find over my head and throw on a fresh pair of sweatpants. Returning to the living room, I snatch my clothes from his hands, pick up my purse, and almost make it out the door.

"No. Nope," Owen says, rushing for the door. He throws his body between me and my last chance to escape an interrogation. "That's not the deal. You owe me an explanation."

"I don't remember making any deal, and I absolutely do not owe you an explanation," I snap back.

He stands stubbornly barring the door. I cock my hip, placing a fist on it.

"I might not be with the sheriff's department, but I'm positive it's a crime to keep a woman against her will." He stares at me angrily for a few minutes before sighing deeply. He moves to the side of the door and motions for me to leave.

"I just don't want to see you get hurt," he says quietly as I scoot past him.

Damn it. I know I'm being a bitch. It's just so embarrassing. My life is embarrassing. The last thing I want to do is explain that to the first man to look at me since I can remember. Instead, I grab the front of his shirt and pull him to me.

Our lips smash against each other. His tongue slides over mine. Someone moans (probably me). It's pure bliss for as long as I allow it to last. But all good things must come to an end. I need to get out of here before I do something we'll regret. Pushing him back against the wall, I take one last lingering look. Then, I slip out the door.

* * *

OWEN

I'm not exactly sure when I lost control of the situation. I think it was somewhere between pulling her out of the bar and watching her hips sway in nothing but a towel.

There is one thing I'm positive about though. She knew exactly what she was doing to knock me off my game. But then after that kiss, I would allow her anything. She threw me a bone, and I caught it like the chump I am.

Speaking of bones. Did she masturbate in my shower? Should I have warned her that the walls in this apartment are paper-thin? I heard her call my name. I was afraid she needed something and started toward the bathroom when I heard a moan. I should have stepped outside to afford her some privacy. Instead, I stood frozen in place.

I'm not sure I would have moved to another room anyway. I can think of few things better than hearing Eliot call out my name when she came. Except maybe being inside her when she does it. Baby steps.

Right now, I have to get to the bottom of whatever is driving her toward self-destruction. There is one person who might be able to give me some insight into it. I pick up my phone.

"Do you have any idea what time it is?" Reed asks when he answers.

"It's like ten."

"Oh. Well, have you seen my fiancée? You'd still be in bed too."

I shake my head. I have seen her. I get it.

"Can you grab a beer later?"

"Sure. We can grab supper while we're at it," Reed agrees. "Just let me know when." He hangs up.

I would call him back just to yell about phone manners, but I could hear sheets rustling in the background. At least one of us is getting some.

With nothing else to do, I collapse onto my bed. Between trying to fit on a couch too short for me and checking that Eliot didn't die of alcohol poisoning, I didn't get much sleep.

My bed smells like Eliot. Sweet, spicy, and just a little sweaty from last night. I inhale deeply. It also has a hint of her perfume still clinging to it. My dick hardens in my jeans. I've been hard off and on since walking into that bar.

Unzipping my jeans, I kick them off on the floor. I can't sleep in jeans anyway. Besides, why should Eliot be the only one in this non-existent relationship to get relief?

Reaching inside my underwear, I fist my erection. What was she thinking walking out in nothing but a towel? My hand moves faster as I remember how the towel skimmed her breasts. If I was a lesser man, that towel would have hit the floor. I would have been on her before she could fight back. But I'm better than that.

My body burns as I think of how she sat in my T-shirt, eating the food I made for her. My hand punishes as I focus on how her breasts felt pressed against me while we kissed.

My body bucks, and I moan her name as I come in my hand. Never in my life have I been this infatuated with a woman. One that challenges me at every turn. One that makes me burn with lust every time I see her.

Climbing off the bed, I walk into the bathroom to clean myself up. The bathroom smells like my soap. Which reminds me of what I heard coming from my shower only a little while ago. My dick twitches. It's going to be a long afternoon.

It takes a while to settle down, but I finally fall asleep around noon. When I wake up, I clean my apartment from top to bottom. I don't usually have time during my shifts to get much done. By the time I'm happy with everything, it's time to meet Reed.

He's already waiting at one of the tables when I walk into the restaurant.

"Hey," he says, shaking my hand. "I hope you don't mind Rand tagging along. He's been kicked out of his house for the evening so the ladies can drink wine and spread rumors. He should be here in a minute."

"Good with me." I take the seat. Reed holds up two fingers to the waitress.

"So I heard a rumor you had a guest sleepover last night," Reed says with a grin.

"That's what I was hoping to talk to you about."

"Damn it, did I miss anything?" Rand asks, sliding into the chair next to me. "I told you to wait for me before discussing who's knocking whose boots."

"No one is knocking anyone's boots," I argue. They both grin at me. They should get out more often.

"Yeah, that's not what's going around town," Rand continues. "I guess Eliot's neighbor saw her walk of shame. She's burned up the phone lines telling everyone about it."

"She could have just been out for an early morning walk," I challenge.

"Except she was wearing a sheriff's department T-shirt."

"Oh." I'm an idiot.

"Was she really singing on the table at the bar? Kevin said she was fair belting it out," Reed asks.

"She was. Do you have any idea why she's doing what she's doing?"

"With Eliot, who knows?" He opens one of the menus. "A burger sounds good."

"That does sound good. I'll have the same," Rand agrees.

"You haven't heard Eliot say anything about what she's

thinking or if something's happened to make what everyone tells me is a reasonably responsible woman act out?"

"My best guess?" Reed says, lowering his voice. I nod. Anything he can tell me would be more than I have right now. "I would guess it has something to do with turning thirty soon. It seems to have her freaking out."

"Seriously? All this is a mid-life crisis?" This is insanity.

twelve

ELIOT

I'VE MANAGED to avoid Owen for almost a week. Not because I particularly want to, but because I've backed myself into a self-imposed corner where we're not quite friends but we're more than polite acquaintances. After all, I don't think I've ever brought up my private parts or gotten off in the shower of a mere acquaintance.

There's also the added nightmare of seeing him around town knowing full well he's the only "friendish" person I have ever kissed like my soul would combust if my lips weren't pressed to his.

"Eliot!" Austen calls from halfway down the street. Did I mention that I feel morally obligated to continue showing up for dance lessons? With any luck, Owen has a shift to work and won't be able to make it tonight. That way, I don't have to spend an evening of torture as his large body presses against mine.

"Hey," I say, reaching my sisters outside the door. "'Sup?"

"So much verbal sophistication, it blows my mind away," Austen teases.

"It's called language conservation; you should try it sometime." Yeah, I don't know if that's a thing.

"Still hungover and sexually frustrated from last weekend, I see," Brontë adds.

"Shut your pie hole," I answer. I spent too many years being threatened with a bar of soap to say what I'm really thinking. Just because not all of us wind up with the hot guy from high school or the sexy billionaire doesn't mean we're sexually frustrated. Okay, so I even rolled my eyes at myself.

"Or we could go inside," Austen suggests. "I'm pretty sure there's a certain deputy that will be relieved you're here. Missi is already doing the feel his arms and comment on how strong he is giggle thing."

I can feel a spike of anger shoot through me. Am I already feeling territorial about a man I'm not even thinking of dating? Well, we have kissed. I'm sure that's made it to the next county over by now. Bitch should have heard about it. Oh, I'm about to cut her for moving in on my territory.

"Jesus, jealous much?" Brontë whispers. "Tone it down, *Fatal Attraction*."

"You don't even know what that movie was about. Besides, I have no claim on him."

"Then stop mumbling about cutting a bitch."

"Can we just dance?" I huff. "Let's do this." I push past my sisters into the room. My gaze immediately finds Owen. Missi has two seconds to remove her hand from his shirt before I remove it for her. Nope. Not my problem.

"I love the enthusiasm," Mrs. Bradford says with a clap. "Everyone find your partners and head out on the floor. If you don't have one, don't worry, we'll find one for you." And because I'm a masochist apparently, I stomp across the room, grab Owen by the wrist, and pull him to the dance floor.

"Wonderful." Mrs. Bradford claps her hands again. "We're going to start with a demonstration of the Latin dances we are learning today. Whenever you're ready, Owen."

My eyes must grow to the size of saucers because he smirks down at me. What have I done? I never agreed to be the other half of his forbidden dance.

"Try to get out of this," he whispers. Then he nods his head and the music starts. Slowly, he runs his hand from the back of my neck down my spine to my ass before pulling me tight against him. I slam against his chest, and he takes the hand I've pressed flat against it. His strong thigh presses between mine.

"Relax your hips," he whispers. Then, we're dancing. Or dry humping, I'm not sure.

"I don't know what I'm doing," I admit quietly.

"Then let me lead you."

His hands travel up and down my body as he turns me exactly how he wants. His hips roll against mine as we move together. Everything slowly disappears around us as he presses his hard planes against my soft curves. We could be anywhere, and I wouldn't notice the people around me. I don't even try to control myself when his hands glide to my waist encouraging me to roll my hips.

This is the most sensual thing I've ever done. He's making me feel like I'm the most desired woman on the planet, like he wants to devour me. And I want him to. I want him to own me in this moment. I want him to roll his hips the same way he would make love to me.

"Excellent." I hear Mrs. Bradford cutting through the lust haze. Everything comes back in a rush as Owen stops, keeping me firmly against him. I look around the group surrounding us. My sisters stand with their mouths open. Reed and Rand have grins on their faces. "So, any questions?"

"No," someone says. "But I'll have what she's having." Everyone laughs and moves onto the dance floor.

"I'm getting a drink." I push out of Owen's arms.

Grabbing a water off the table on the way by, I stumble back outside. I can use a couple of breaths of fresh air too. I pop my bottle open and lean against the wall. If I had an old-fashioned hand fan, I'd be fanning.

"Are you okay?" Owen asks, stepping outside.

"No."

"What's wrong?" His eyebrows scrunch in the middle.

"What's wrong, you ask?" I sputter. "I think my vagina just caught fire." He tries to hide his laugh by coughing, but I catch it. "It's not funny. I might be ruined to all but sexy Latin men. What was that?"

"It's called bachata. It's a little too advanced for this crowd, but I've always wanted to try it. For obvious reasons, my mom never taught it." I look up at him. "You know, because of the whole flaming vagina and everything."

I can't help it. I laugh. Then I bang against him, and he laughs. Who discusses their turned-on lady parts with a random guy friend? He didn't even flinch this time. I've brought him over to the dark side.

"Should we go back inside and show them how to mambo?" He holds out his elbow for me to take. "I promise no burning lady bits. Unless you like that."

"I say yes to showing up those bitches." I take his elbow.

"I'll let you know about those flaming bits." We both grin and open the door to make our dramatic re-entry.

* * *

OWEN

If she thinks learning how to dance a handful of Latin numbers is lady bit combusting (her words, not mine), wait until I jump, jive, and wail her. I should start lifting more at the gym. I wonder if I can convince her to keep dancing with me after the lessons are done. Right now, I'm trying to convince her it's okay to roll those hips. I'm fighting an uphill battle.

"You have to move your hips like a belly dancer," I try.

"You've got to let my hips do what they want. You're not the boss of them."

"Fine." I spin her to me, shove her crotch against my thigh, and do a merengue dip. I snap her back up to my chest. She tries to move away, but I hold her fast.

"Now, move with me." I over-exaggerate my hips, holding her tight against me. It takes a minute, but finally, she relaxes into an impressive hip rock that anyone would envy. "Better."

"If you're getting tired, Eliot, I'll be happy to trade," the woman who draped herself on me before Eliot arrived says when she dances by holding on to a man that can't be younger than eighty if he's a day. Eliot spins around so she's backed up against me. She bends slightly and executes an impressive grind roll.

"I'm sure I can grind against his cock as good as you can," she hisses. The other woman rolls her eyes and dances away with gramps in tow. Eliot has no problem swinging her hips now. And if we were in private, I'd be all for it.

"You're going to have to stop doing that, or we'll have to take this to the back alley."

"Oh," she says, spinning back around to face me. "Sorry. My bad."

"Yeah," I say, rolling my eyes.

The music changes to a rumba. What is this dance teacher thinking? This is going to be a whole room of sore people tomorrow. The instructor begins explaining the dance. I tune her out since I can do this one already.

"Remember to keep your hips moving. Follow my lead." She nods, and I take her hand.

"This might be the best workout in town. Is this how you stayed fit growing up?"

"It's part of it. I did other things too."

"Like?"

"I played hockey. I ran track. I boxed. The police academy was no walk in the park."

"A regular Ironman."

"I wouldn't go that far." She smiles up at me as we finish our dance.

The instructor has suggested that I change partners occasionally. It would help some of the women struggling to learn the steps, she said. I can't seem to pry myself away from Eliot however. Every time we part, all I can think about is when I'll see her again. If I have to use dance class to hold her, I'm not trading that for anyone.

"Okay, that's all for tonight. Wonderful work, everyone. Until next week," our instructor says. Couples part ways to gather their things. I'm reluctant to let Eliot go. I worry if it'll be another week before I'm allowed to see her again. Unless I'm arresting her for the next prank gone wrong.

"Thank you for being my partner again this week," I say.

"Hey, a deal's a deal." Not exactly what I was hoping to hear. "Want to grab something to eat? We were planning on grabbing pizza."

"Sure." It's not like I'm going to pass up a chance to spend even more time with her. We're joined by not only her sisters and their significant others, but a handful of their friends as well. We manage to overwhelm the single employee in the pizza place almost immediately.

"Brontë," the older gentleman behind the counter yells. "See what everyone wants, and I'll start prepping dough."

"I got ya, Mr. Barron," she hollers back. Standing, she grabs an order pad from behind the counter and starts writing down pizza orders.

"She worked here in high school," Eliot says when I slide into the booth next to her. "He forgets she's not fifteen anymore." She winks and turns to her sister. "Waitress, I'd like to order my drink. I'll have soda; thirty-three percent Coke, twenty-two percent Pepsi, twelve percent diet."

"You'll drink what I give you and be grateful I didn't spit in it," Brontë answers. "Owen?"

"Coke and meat lovers," I answer.

"Meat lovers? How about some vegetables also?" Eliot says.

"With mushrooms and tomatoes?"

"Don't let her bully you," Austen chastises me.

"It's fine. I like vegetables."

"Damn, you're already whipped," Reed says.

"Without getting any p—"

"Rand!" the women yell together. Reed holds out his fist, and Rand bumps it.

"Eliot, what pizza do you want?" She looks around like an idea will pop out of the walls.

"I'm fine. I'll just stick with my drink."

"You're not dieting again, are you?" Austen asks. Eliot's face blushes, and she sneaks a peek at me. I wish she could see herself as I see her. She's perfect with curves in all the right places.

"How about making mine a large?" I suggest. "You can share with me. I'll take home what we don't finish."

"But just pepperoni and bacon, no sausage," she adds, and Brontë moves on. Reed makes a whip-cracking noise. There are more fist bumps.

"So, let's talk about you showing us up on the dance floor," Reed says, steering the conversation in a different direction. "I think I might have gotten pregnant watching that first one tonight." I laugh, and we fall into an easy conversation. It's nice to finally have a group I can go out to pizza with.

It's an hour before anyone is willing to head home. When Eliot finally leaves, I follow to walk her home. We have to walk by my apartment on the way. There's an alley that runs beside it that we cut through to her house.

"Would you like to come up?" I ask. She cocks her head at me then shifts her gaze to my apartment door.

"I can't imagine why you want to spend any more time with me than necessary."

"Maybe you're right." I pull her to a stop. "Why would I want to spend time with someone funny, brilliant, clever, and beautiful? It's a real hardship, let me tell you." I don't give her a chance to argue. My hand slides to the nape of her neck, and I pull her against me. "A real hardship," I mutter right before our lips meet.

If kissing Eliot is a hardship, I'll take hardship all day

any day. Her lips are soft and taste like the cherry vanilla lip balm she carries in her purse. My tongue traces the seam of her lips, and she opens her mouth in invitation. It doesn't slip my mind that there is so much more of her I'd like to explore with my tongue.

I could continue this forever, except we have to breathe. Taking a step back, I stare down into her golden gaze daring me to go back for more. Unfortunately, my elderly landlord pulls into the driveway. It seems like something is always keeping us at arm's length.

"Owen," Mrs. Marquez calls. "Can you help me with the groceries? Oh, hello, Eliot." As much as I want to ignore her and focus all my attention on Eliot, I was raised better.

"You could wait upstairs for me," I suggest.

"I should head home," she answers. With a wave, she continues toward her house. I watch her hips sway until she turns the corner. I sigh and turn back to the task at hand. I'm not sure this slow-burn romance can get any slower and I survive.

thirteen

OWEN

I BET you expect me to run to Eliot's house, pound on her door, and profess that I can't live another minute without her. I guess I can, but that seems a little far-fetched.

Instead, I carry my landlady's groceries inside. Then, I take a long shower, mostly because working that hard to look good on the dance floor left me smelling less than favorable.

Would I like for tonight to have gone differently? Of course. But there will be another opportunity. This game of cat and mouse is just heating up.

I find out just how hot it's getting two days later when I receive a call while on parole.

"Owen, what's your twenty?" Cherylynn calls over the radio.

"I'm at the gas station."

"Can you head on over to the pool? We got a silent alarm from there."

"Yeah, I'll swing over." I drive to the pool and pull up near the park office.

The only way to access the town swimming pool is through the front of the building where the park department office is. Inside, there's a small meeting room, lockers, and bathrooms beside the main office. During the summer, they open one of the exterior gates to divert the kids through.

I try the door, but it's locked. Fortunately, I have a master key to the city offices. I find the right one and slip it into the lock. It doesn't take me long to work through the building. No one is lurking in any of the indoor spaces. That only leaves one other place to check. I push through the glass door to the pool.

Standing at the edge of the pool, staring into the water, is Eliot. I should have known. "What are you doing?" I ask, making her jump.

"I have permission to be in here from Brian. He gave me the keys so I could use the pool."

"To do what?" Her face turns a delicious shade of red, and I can't wait to hear what's next.

"Skinny dip?" She finally rolls her eyes and steps back. "It's on my list."

"What fucking list?" I say in frustration. I've been trying for weeks now to get an answer for her crazy behavior.

"The list of things I need to do before I turn thirty," she snaps back. Now I'm even more confused.

"What happens at thirty?"

"Everything, nothing," she yells. Then her body just seems to collapse in on itself. "Oh, what's the use? I'm destined to just grow old having done nothing exciting in life. My youth will be over, and I can start collecting cats."

I bark out a laugh. I can't help it.

"So everything ends at thirty. Is that what you're saying?"

"Might as well be. Life is supposed to be full of adventure and risk when you're young. Then at thirty, you slow down. Start a family, buy a house, start a business. I missed all of that first part and went straight for the old people things."

"So if you hit thirty without having all of those things, you must be a loser?" I ask. "I'm thirty-four and don't have any of those things. Maybe someday, but not yet. Does that make me a loser?"

"No," she says quickly. "I didn't mean you. I bet you did all kinds of crazy things when you were younger. Not me. I studied and then worked. That's it." Suddenly, all of her antics are starting to make more sense to me.

"And you believe that if you do all of these things, you won't have wasted your youth?"

"I know it sounds stupid, but it's sort of like a bucket list. Things to do before you die. Or turn thirty which is the same thing." I shake my head. She's crazy, but something about her kind of crazy makes me want to jump on board.

"It's not stupid." I look around the pool. There is a privacy fence around the outside, so no one should be able to see inside. She's also left most of the lights off. It's a bright night, so there's plenty of ambient light. "Okay, let's do this."

"Wait. Do what?" Her eyes grow wide when I slip off my gun belt. My shirt follows next. I'm officially off duty now. I was heading home when I got this last call. I shove my shoes and socks under one of the lounge chairs.

"Are you getting in?" I ask, pushing my pants down my legs.

"Mmm-hmm." Her mouth is slightly open as her gaze

explores my body. I'd smirk, but I'm afraid I'll destroy the moment. In the very basic sense, this is what I've been angling for. Eliot. Me. Naked.

"Get going. We've got swimming to do." I turn my back to her, slide off my underwear, and dive into the pool.

When I emerge, Eliot has her back to me, peeling off her clothes. I turn around to give her some privacy. It's hard. I'd like to feast on naked Eliot in so many ways. I hear a splash and turn around right as her head pops back out of the water.

"It's cold," she squeals.

"It is," I agree with a grin. "Have you never skinny-dipped before?"

"Never. It feels amazing." She starts to float on her back before remembering she's still naked. I watch her flounder around trying to get her body back under the water.

"Come here." I hold out my hand.

She's hesitant but finally swims to me. I can reach the bottom of the pool where we're at; she can't. When she draws close enough, I gently slide my hand behind her neck and pull her against me. Her body feels so amazing against mine that I have to close my eyes to maintain control.

Gently, I spin her in my arms and lay her head on my shoulder. Her body slowly floats to the surface as she relaxes. The water is like a curtain slowly opening on a hidden gem.

I ease her arms out to the side as she gazes up at the stars. That is one of the best things about living in a small town; the stars are visible even in the middle of town.

"Beautiful," I whisper in her ear.

"They are."

"I wasn't talking about the stars." She smiles, and my heart kicks up a beat. It's the perfect night. The sky is clear, the stars fill the night sky, and I have the most stunning woman with me. Nothing could ruin this night.

"Owen?"

"Shit," I bark, scrambling to shove Eliot back under the water. I get her pressed up behind me just as Arlo comes striding into the pool area.

"Hey, we've been trying to get you on the... oh." His gaze traces over the stack of clothes on the lounger. Then they cut to Eliot's clothes. "Hey, Eliot." He gives me a shit-eating grin.

"Hey, Arlo," she says, peering over my shoulder.

"I'll just let the office know you're fine." He smirks at me. "Want me to lock the door on the way out?"

"Yes," I growl between clenched teeth.

"You kids have fun." With a wave, he's gone.

"What do you think the chance he won't tell everyone in town that he saw us skinny dipping is?" Eliot asks, still clinging to my back.

"You've lived here your whole life, you tell me."

I'm pissed. Everything was going so perfectly. I should have called back in when everything was clear. The universe keeps conspiring to keep us apart. Well, you know what? Fuck the universe.

"I guess we should go. I'd hate to be busted twice in one night." She pushes away from me.

"Eliot—"

"Do you—" she begins. I hold my tongue as she looks back up at the sky. When she looks back down at me something in her has changed. Her gaze is on fire like she's finally settled on a decision she's been wrestling with. "Do you want to come to my place? It's such a nice night I hate to waste it."

"I'd love to come over." I can feel her gaze on me as I lift myself out of the pool. I redress and carry the towel to the end of the pool she's at. I hold it open waiting to see if she'll come take it from me. She doesn't hesitate as she stands and faces me.

She owns the pool as she walks through the shallow end. My chest starts to heave and my heart hammers in my ears as her body slowly emerges from the water. Her skin is alabaster, her nipples a soft pink, and her hips flare in the perfect handhold.

I would close my eyes again to recapture my control, but I don't want to miss a minute. She slowly wraps the towel around her before gliding to her clothes.

"Jesus," I whisper. She gives me a saucy look over her shoulder. I moan and turn toward the door. If I don't leave right now, neither one of us is leaving anytime soon.

I move through the rooms making sure no one other than Arlo came in while we were in the pool. Slumping onto a bench in the foyer, I wait for Eliot to appear.

"Ready," she says, stepping around the corner.

"You have no idea."

* * *

ELIOT

I can't believe I did that. It's one thing to walk around naked when you're cut like a marble statue like Owen. It's another to do it with hips that are a little too round, a stomach a little too soft, and breasts that are already debating their downward plunge. But the way he held out the towel was like a dare. And the new young and wild me wanted to take that dare.

That side of me is long gone as I sit in his cruiser for the short trip to my house. I can't think of anything to say so I'm just staring out the window in silence. I chance a glance at Owen. He doesn't seem uncomfortable with the silence. He has a small smile on his face.

"What are you thinking about?" I ask when I can't stand it anymore.

"I was thinking that of all your escapades, this one was by far my favorite." I turn to the window so he can't see my grin. It was my favorite so far too. When I'm back under control, I turn back around.

"So, what you're saying is getting shot with a Roman candle wasn't at the top of your list?"

"I'd say getting shot by a rocket ranks just below colonoscopy."

"But just above eating a slug."

"Have you eaten a lot of slugs?" He laughs, and I feel myself relaxing.

"One time in elementary, Josh McGuire held me down and made me eat one."

"Do you want me to hunt him down and teach him how to treat a woman?" he asks.

"Nah, I've moved past it." He laughs again as we pull up to my house.

The minute of confidence I felt is wiped out. My nerves ratchet back up to a critical level. What was I thinking inviting him to the house? He turns off his cruiser and hops out. Apparently, he's not freaking out like I am. He opens my door.

"Are you still okay with me being here?"

"Of course. Why wouldn't I be?" Yeah, that sounded impressively cool. I can do this. I'm the new and improved Eliot Caraway after all. He follows me to my door. Every scenario that can happen once we're inside flashes through my mind.

"Would you like something to drink?"

"Sure." He wanders into the living area. My kitchen, dining room, and living room are just one large room divided by furniture. I bought it five years ago. It needed some work that I've slowly been finishing, but I love it.

I open two beers and carry them across the room. Owen is sitting on my couch with his legs stretched in front of him.

As far as I see it I have two choices at this point. I can hand him the beer, and we can go out back to stare at the stars. Or, and I like this idea slightly better, I can straddle those long legs.

The way he held me in the pool while I stared at the stars lit a flame in me so hot it's threatening to melt me. Standing in front of him, I weigh my choices. His dark gaze meets mine like he knows what I'm struggling with.

Slowly, he pulls his legs up providing me with a tempting platform. I hand him a beer as I slide onto his legs. He tips his head back for a long drink. I watch as his Adam's apple bobs up and down. He takes my beer out of my hand, setting them both on the coffee table. His strong hands caress my bottom before pulling me to him. I crash against his chest with a gasp.

"I've been wanting to do this all night," he says. His lips move toward mine, and I meet him halfway, just as anxious to taste him as he is me. Our tongues slide against each other.

There's no going back. My fingers shake as they attack the buttons on his shirt. I need it off quickly. I need to feast on all that muscle I saw in the pool.

"I need you naked," I moan. I've never said that to a

man. I'm not a complete prude; I've had sex before. But I've never needed it like I do now. In the past, it was just the next step in dating. Tonight, with Owen, it's like I won't survive without it. He lets me shove his shirt off his shoulders.

My hands roam over his shoulders, down his abs, to his belt. It's like I've lost everything but the primal need to feel him inside me.

I don't bother to pull his belt from its loops. Instead, I fight with the button on his pants. He lifts his hips for me when I finally have them open. His cock springs up hard and hot against his abdomen. My hand wraps around it.

"Easy," he moans. I pump once then release it.

"Do you have a condom?" I ask.

"In my wallet." I find it and toss it toward him.

"Put it on. Quickly." My gaze can't seem to leave him. I stare, mesmerized, at him while I undress.

"You're stunning," he says when I slide back on his lap. I'd like to believe him. I'm trying to. I open my mouth to argue, but he pulls one of my nipples between his lips.

My body clenches. No, I'm not having an orgasm without him inside me. His hand slides down and finds my clit. My body warns me again when he slides his fingers through my folds until they are seated deep inside me.

"You're going to make me come," I gasp.

"Several times if I have my way," he answers.

"Later. You can do all the things later." I bat his hands away. Gripping his cock, I line it up where I'm on fire and slide down on it. We both swear. I'm so close I worry I won't last very long. That doesn't seem to matter to Owen though. When my hips begin to rock, he encourages me on with his hands.

"Oh my god," I moan. I've never had an orgasm without

some external help. But this isn't just sex. Something is happening between us that's not happened in the past.

I ride him like he's the last bull at the rodeo. Then I'm soaring. I'm weightless as I float around the room. All I can hear is the sound of wind in my ears. I feel like I'm looking through gauze. I hear Owen say something, but nothing makes sense.

My mind clears, and I'm lying against his chest. I can hear his heart pounding in his chest. I might have blacked out; I'm not sure yet. Owen is running his hand down the back of my hair.

Never when I shot the sheriff did I think I'd wind up on top of him. I know that my list of things to do before old age sounds stupid, but I'm grateful for it. Without that list... Well, let's not think about that.

fourteen

OWEN

I KNOW Eliot thinks of what we did as a one-night stand. That's obvious by the way she hasn't returned my calls or texts. But rest assured, it was not.

I'm letting her run through the five stages of freakout. I'm not sure what those stages are, but with her, they're sure to take a little while. I don't think if I have her the rest of my life, I'll ever work out the mystery that is Eliot Caraway.

I worked the morning shift in the pouring rain. It's been raining since yesterday, and everything is muddy. I managed to drag a couple of high school kids out of their Jon boat right before they launched it into the swelling river.

Old Mrs. Woods had me check her attic, positive someone was living up there. There was, of the tree climbing four-footed variety. I turned the problem over to Coit, the government trapper and animal control guy.

My entire day continued in the same way. By the time I

pull up to my apartment, I'm soaked. The rain has stopped at least. I climb out of my cruiser debating if I should leave the window down so it can dry out when a jumped-up Jeep pulls up next to me. Who do I know that drives a Jeep?

"Let's go, po-po," Eliot calls. I scowl at her. Either she's worked through the panic steps quick or she's on step five, desperately trying to put me in the friend zone. That's not going to happen. "What? Get in."

"Can I change into dry clothes first?"

"If that's what gets you moving." I roll my eyes but head up the stairs. It takes me five minutes to change into dry clothes. When I return to the Jeep, Eliot has trash metal screaming through the stereo system. All I can think is that I must have lost my damn mind to get in the passenger seat next to her.

"Fasten your seat belts; it's going to be a bumpy night," she says in her best Bette Davis voice.

This is when I should dive from the vehicle, but a part of me yearns to find out what she's got in mind this time. I've become addicted to Eliot. I'm not ashamed to admit it. I open my mouth to ask where we're going, but before I can, she spins out of my driveway heading out of town.

She drives about fifteen minutes then cuts back down a road that leads to the river. She slides to a stop when we top a hill, and I see exactly how the town of Dansboro Crossing occupies itself on a late rainy afternoon.

Zipping around in the sandy mud is every form of off-road vehicle imaginable. From large go-karts to jacked-up Jeeps, they all have one thing in common. They're all covered in mud.

She slaps a pair of goggles against my chest. I don't even have time to react before I hear a warrior princess scream, and we're hurtling toward the river. I think the scream came from Eliot, but no promises.

This Jeep has no roof, no doors, no front windshield. It takes her less than five seconds of sliding through the mud to completely cover me in it.

"Isn't this amazing?" she yells at me as she aims toward a giant mound of dirt.

I grab on to anything I can find as we fly into the air. The wheels hit with a bounce. She slides an impressive J-turn, and we're heading the other way. I don't have time to wonder how all of these vehicles manage to avoid running into each other before we're in the air again.

"Eliot!" I scream, but she's already got us doing donuts. When we come to a stop, her gaze homes in on mine. Her eyes flash, and we're off again. She quickly arrives at the end of the muddy area. Drifting the Jeep around, we head in again. I didn't even know you could do that in a Jeep and not flip it over. I think she missed her calling.

We do the entire course twice more before she slides to a stop. She looks at me and grins through muddy lips. I understand now why she brought us goggles. Our eyes are the only part of either of us you can still identify.

"You want a turn?" she asks. I hesitate for a whole second before I answer.

"Hell, yes." We grin at each other and then race around the Jeep.

Settling into the driver's side, I wait until Eliot is set, then let out my own war cry. I've decided halfway up the first jump that I might have just killed us both. But we land more or less safely. I make two rounds of the course. My adrenaline is at an all-time high.

"Is there anywhere a little more private?" I yell.

"Down the river, it becomes rocky. No one drives down there."

I nod and head down the river. The noise softens as we bounce over rocks looking to leave the others behind. Soon, we can't hear the free-for-all going on not far away. I stop the Jeep and turn off the engine. I gaze over at Eliot; she gazes back at me. Suddenly, we're both scrambling out of the Jeep.

"Condom?" she asks breathlessly.

I fish my wallet out of the glove compartment. It's thankfully clean. Fishing a condom from it, I return to the front of the Jeep in three quick steps. My hands go to her messy hair bringing her close. Our lips meet, and I don't care if they are muddy. Nothing will keep me from her.

My hands travel to her waistband. I wrestle with the button on her jeans before I have to end the kiss and drop to my knees. I finally get them open so I can peel them down her legs.

The plan is to stand back up, but that's before she gasps as I slide my fingers back up her thighs. Grabbing her panties, I twist the lace until they rip. Her breath turns to shallow pants.

I help her off with her shoes and pants before I pull one leg over my shoulder.

"Owen," she moans as my tongue finds her folds.

Nothing tastes as good as Eliot. Her hand wraps in my hair as I explore. She hisses when I gently suck on her clit. She rocks against my face when I flick it with my tongue.

Pulling her other leg on my shoulder, I lift her onto the hood of the Jeep. I spread her legs wide so I could plunge my tongue inside. She moans when I flatten it against her clit. It doesn't take long before I feel the thighs next to my head start to shake. Her back arches, and she screams. She's a screamer. Damn, that's hot.

I step back with a grin as she comes down. "I didn't know you're a screamer." She sits up on the hood, her eyes slightly glazed from the orgasm.

"I didn't know either. Should we make sure?" She holds out the condom package. I put it between my teeth while I wrestle down my muddy jeans. I rip the package open, slide the condom down my shaft, and pull her off the hood.

Her heat encases my length perfectly. I'm not gentle like I tried to be last time. This is going to be hot and dirty. Literally.

My first thrust makes her gasp, but I'm looking for a scream again. With her pressed against the grill of the Jeep, I bounce her on my cock.

"Come on, Eliot. I want to hear you scream," I whisper in her ear.

She moans and grinds her hips with every thrust. I can feel lava making its way up my spine. I need her to finish before I do. I drive even harder into her. At this pace, I'm not going to be able to hold out.

Then she clenches around me, and a string of obscenities flows from her mouth. I would think more about that, but instead, I have that sensation of floating as my cock pulses inside her.

My arms are wrapped around her, holding her slick body tight to mine. We're muddy, should be charged with public indecency, and I couldn't be happier.

"I believe someone needs their mouth washed out with soap," I tease. I've grown soft, but I'm not ready yet to turn her loose. She hasn't pushed me away either.

"I was trying to enlarge your vocabulary. Did it work?"

"I certainly learned new ways to describe what we just did."

"Then my job here is done," she declares.

I laugh and slowly lower her to her feet. After pulling my jeans up, I hold hers so she can step into them. It takes a joint effort to wrestle them back up her luscious legs. I carry her to the passenger seat of the Jeep where she pulls back on her boots.

"Are you ready to go? I'm starving," I say.

"Yeah, I could use something to eat too. I rushed straight from work to pick you up."

"Where did you get the Jeep? No, let me guess. Cam lent it to you."

"She's awesome like that."

"Remind me to have a conversation with her about lending vehicles to delinquents." I start the Jeep and start the bounce back to the main road. "You might not mention I was with you either. I don't want any trouble from Sheriff Rogers."

"You're fine. Wes comes out here all the time after it rains." I'm not sure what I think about that. Small towns are definitely different.

"So, do you want me to drop you off?" I ask.

"Nah," she says with a wink. "I've already messed up the one-night stand on my list. You should just come shower with me. Then we'll order pizza."

I can't help the giant grin on my face. Her ideas just get better and better. Predictably, I drive back to town as fast as I can without risking a ticket. I know I'm excited to get back to town and Eliot into the shower.

"Do you mind if we swing by my place so I can grab a change of clothes?"

"Of course. Though, I'm thinking you don't need

clothes for what I have in mind." I stomp on the gas pedal a little harder. Ticket be damned.

We're back in town in record time. I'm still swinging by my place, hoping the clothes I grab aren't needed until tomorrow. I pull up to my apartment and freeze.

"What the hell?" It takes all my concentration to put the Jeep in park. Slowly, I climb out of the driver's seat.

"What's wrong?" I don't answer as I walk toward the skinny girl standing on my stairs.

"Tess?" The girl gives me a small wave. "How long have you been here?"

"Not long, I promise," she answers.

"Where's your mom?"

"She has a new boyfriend, and he doesn't like kids, and she said I'm better off here anyway. Can I please stay? I promise I won't be any trouble," she blurts out.

"Tess, you know you are always welcome to stay here. But I need to talk to your mom."

"She sent a bunch of papers for you." She sits down on the step and starts rummaging through her backpack.

"How about I clean up and get us something to eat first, kiddo? How's that sound?" I swear I can hear her stomach growl from over here. "Maybe my friend can join us?" I turn around to invite Eliot for pizza and to meet Tessa, but she's gone.

"She left. I'm sorry, Uncle Owen."

"Nothing to be sorry for. I'm sure she wanted to get the mud washed off as much as I do. Let's get inside." I pull my keys out of my muddy pocket and open the door. Tessa shuffles inside behind me. "I'll run through the shower. Be thinking about what kind of pizza you want."

I pull my phone out the second the bathroom door closes. Eliot's phone goes right to voicemail. I hope that just means she's in the shower and not pissed at me. I decide just to send a simple message.

Owen: Sorry. Rain check?

The mess that is my sister needs to be explained in person, not over a text message. Peeling my jeans off, I make a muddy pile on the floor. My mind whirls thinking about what I'm going to do with Tessa. She's come in and out of my life since she was born based on my sister's whims.

By the time I've washed all the mud down the drain, I've decided it's time for Tessa to have a forever home, and if her mother won't provide it, then I will.

"Hey, have you decided what pizza you want?" I ask when I walk back into the living room. Tessa is slumped on the couch watching television.

"Whatever you want, Uncle Owen."

"So if I get anchovy and green pepper, you're good with that?"

Her nose scrunches in disgust.

"Or artichoke and broccoli?"

"Gross." She laughs. That's the bright sunny girl I remember. "Can we just get pepperoni?"

"Pepperoni it is."

"And soda?" she asks hopefully.

"And water or milk. I'm not that soft of a touch."

She slouches back on the couch to continue her show, but I can see a smile fighting at the corner of her mouth. I'm worried about what's happened in the year since I saw her last. Did any money go into feeding her, or did my sister use most of it to feed her habit? Did the boyfriend slap Tessa around, or worse?

I pull out the packet of papers while she's occupied watching television. I have to do a double take at the second paper. It's the form voluntarily giving up my sister's maternal rights. I'll still have to get a judge to issue a court order, but it's a start.

I debate if I tell Tessa I'm going to begin adoption proceedings. No twelve-year-old should have to deal with being bounced through the court system. The judge might, however, require her to appear in court to answer questions.

As much as I don't want to hurt her any more than her mother already has, this is a conversation that needs to happen now. With a sigh, I move to the couch.

fifteen

ELIOT

I DON'T KNOW what to think. Yeah, I know he's complicated and probably bad for me, but I can't keep away. And the sex on the Jeep? Holy craptastic. Never have I had sex on the hood of any vehicle. I know that we're just now getting to know each other, but you'd think the fact he has a daughter would have come up in conversation. Before he seduced me onto the hood preferably.

"So the rumors are true." I try to ignore Austen's voice.

"I told you she was Girls Gone Wild, Dansboro Crossing style." Great, they're both here. I spray the hose at the Jeep again, dislodging more mud. Cam's only condition was that I return it clean.

"Rumor has it," Brontë continues, "that you went mudding with a mysterious passenger and disappeared for half an hour. Like to expound on that?"

I ignore them both. Tossing the sprayer hose on the lawn, I head for my house. Unfortunately, they follow. Little sisters are such pests.

"You're welcome," Austen says, closing the door a few minutes later. "I turned off the water."

Before I can even roll my eyes, Brontë pipes up.

"Don't you think there are more important things right now than if Eliot depletes the town's water supply? Like the rumor they were just gone long enough to thread that needle."

"Just to set the record straight, my hose has an attachment on it that shuts off if I'm not pressing it. No one is getting dehydrated on my watch. And it was more like greasing the pole," I snap back.

Looking up, I fully expect my sisters to be horrified with me. Instead, they both have giant, stupid grins on their faces. Then they let out some kind of keening noise that I guess is supposed to show their excitement.

"Dog!" Brontë yells, pointing at me.

"Tell us everything," Austen says. She's bouncing on the couch like a four-year-old on Christmas morning. "Did you seduce him? Did he use his handcuffs? Do you call him officer? Does he insist on slow and easy or fast and rough?" She's giving me a headache. Brontë just nods her head faster with every question. "Does he make you scream?"

"Umm."

Oh, my god, Brontë mouths at Austen.

"Our big sister has herself a side piece," Austen adds.

"I think you have to have a main piece to have a side piece," Brontë points out.

"I was trying to make a sheriff reference. You know, like their guns are a side piece?"

"I guess. Ooh, I bet he hauled you in the first time just to get your number."

"No, he hauled me in because I shot him with a Roman candle," I remind her.

"Still. What did he say the first time he saw you? Was he flirting?" Brontë continues.

"He said 'Ma'am.' Then I shot him. Not super romantic. Oh, then he insulted my name."

"So right up there with me breaking Reed's nose then," Austen replies. "Looks like Brontë's drunken one-night stand might have been the least deadly way to meet a man."

"I'd give two thumbs up to getting knocked up by your one-night stand to get the ball rolling," Brontë replies snidely. She rolls her eyes.

"Do we get to tell everyone now that y'all are an item?" Austen asks.

"I don't think so."

"Why? What happened?"

"Everything was good. But yesterday when we got back, a young girl was waiting for him that he obviously has a history with. Has to be his daughter."

"That doesn't sound like a deal breaker," Brontë says. "I have a kid, and Rand still wanted me."

"It was Rand's kid," I point out.

"Semantics." She grins at me. "I'm just busting your lady balls. Still, what's the problem with him having a kid?"

"Nothing, except you would have thought he would have mentioned it."

"I'm arresting you for being a public nuisance. By the way, I have a daughter that may be left on my doorstep. Is that what you're looking for?"

"No. I don't know. Maybe just a heads up." I don't like this conversation. I haven't had time to process what I saw.

Yesterday, after I got home, I showered, ate some leftovers, watched too many movies, and fell asleep on the couch. This morning, I scrubbed my house and worked on the Jeep. Anything to keep from having to figure out what's going on with Owen.

"How about we take you to lunch? We can talk it out over wine," Austen says, wrapping her arms around me.

"Or we could do tacos and margaritas at the new place?" Brontë says, doing the same from the other side.

"If I say yes, will it get y'all out of my house for the rest of the day?" I ask.

"Scout's honor."

"Promise."

"Then I'm thinking tequila. Let's go." I stand. They follow me out the door. I know I bitch about them a lot, but there is a chance they're exactly who I need right now. If anyone can shed light on a complicated situation, it's my sisters. "Wait, you can't have tequila."

"Thanks for raining on the parade," Brontë answers. "I also know that."

"I'm sure we can day-drink for her too," Austen assures me as we reach her car. "Besides, I've heard their margs are worth the headache."

"Sounds like a plan."

* * *

OWEN

I'm so overwhelmed I don't know if I'm coming or going. Deciding to file for sole custody of Tessa has started a mountain of red tape I have to work through.

I got the court order I needed from the judge for temporary custody until Child Protective Services has finished their investigation into if I'll be a fit guardian. The paperwork from my sister signing over her rights will help, they say.

We spent Sunday converting my bedroom into Tessa's bedroom. I'll be on the couch for the foreseeable future. We'll have to share the closet and bathroom until I can find somewhere else. Finding rental houses in a small town is not as easy as you think. At least she has a room she can call her own for now.

I had to call in sick to work on Sunday. Monday, I went and threw myself at the mercy of Sheriff Rogers. He smiled, gave me the week off paid, and offered to help me start hunting for new housing. There are certainly some pluses to living in a small town too. As soon as I can find flexible childcare, I'll be ready to work extra shifts to make up for what everyone else is doing for me.

I tried to register Tessa in school on Tuesday, but her vaccine records were incomplete. So on Wednesday, I took her to Fredericksburg for her twelve-year boosters.

We grabbed some new school clothes and supplies while we were there. She informed me that, coupled with the ice cream I bought, she guessed she'd forgive me for the shots.

Now it's Thursday, and we're about to make another run at the school. A million things are flying through my head as we cross town. I'm so deep in thought that it takes Tessa several times calling my name to hear her.

"Uncle Owen!"

"What? What's up, buttercup?" She rolls her eyes but quickly grows serious again.

"Who were you with?"

"What are you talking about?" So much has happened it could be almost anyone.

"That woman? She was all muddy like you. You were in that big Jeep."

"Oh, that was a friend."

"What's your friend's name?"

"Eliot," I say with a smile. It's the only way I can say her name.

"Is she your girlfriend?"

Is she? I adore everything about her. Even when she's behaving badly. That might be when I like her best. I can't think of anyone I'd rather spend my time with. She's funny in a dry-humor way. She's smart as a whip and knows how to turn a phrase. And my heart races when I see her. It sounds like the very definition of a girlfriend.

"Yes?"

"Do you not want her to meet me? Will she not like me?" I almost slide the cruiser to a stop in the middle of the street, but I manage to keep it moving.

"No, Tess. I think she'll love you. And I know you'll adore her. She's really fun. Everything has just been so crazy I haven't had time to invite her over to meet you." We pull up in front of the school. "Let's see if they'll let you in today."

"Okay." She nods and climbs out of the car.

That's another thing I need to do. I need to track down Eliot. She deserves an explanation about Tessa and why I've turned into the ghost this time. The fact she has never responded to my brief texts says a lot. But I have to put everything except for what I have to do next out of my brain.

"Hi," I say to the secretary when we finally make it through the security into the middle school. "I'm not sure if you remember us. We were here Tuesday—"

"Officer Steele," she says, cutting me off. "Have everything together this time?"

"I hope so."

"Good. If you'll have a seat, Ms. Scott would like to visit with you."

Crap, I've already been called into the principal's office and I don't even go to school here.

"Tessa, would you like one of our students to show you around? Colton is in your grade. He's one of our new student ambassadors. He'll answer any questions you might have."

My niece nods.

The secretary calls down to a classroom, and soon a too-good-looking-for-his-own good kid shows up. He's tall for his age with perfect white teeth. His hair even sweeps artfully over his brow like every teen movie star wishes for.

Where did they get this kid? Did he walk off of a movie set? There's no way he's twelve. He introduces himself to Tessa. She giggles and follows him out the door.

"His last name's not Campbell, is it?" I ask with a scowl. "Couldn't find a girl to show her around?"

"Officer Steele?" a woman standing just inside the door to the principal's office asks. I take one last look down the hallway through the glass window at my niece. She's happily hanging on every smile thrown her way. Double crap.

"I'm Principal Scott." I'm forced to turn and shake her hand.

"Very nice to meet you. Is there a problem with Tessa's enrollment?"

"Not at all." She motions me inside her office. Closing the door behind her, she returns to the large leather chair behind her desk. I take the chair closest to me. "I just want to make sure we have everything under control for Tessa's safety. I understand you have temporary full custody, and there is a restraining order?"

"Yes. I included everything in the paperwork, including a photo of her mother. In the past, her mother would simply pick her up and disappear. I want to make sure that doesn't happen this time," I answer.

"And this is her mother, Gwyn Steele?" She holds up the photo of my sister.

"The most recent one I have."

"Is there anyone else she might get to lure Tessa away?"

"I don't know. I don't think Tessa would go with anyone else."

"Good. Rest assured, Officer Steele, we will do everything within our power to keep her safe while at school. I'll make sure the teachers are made aware on Friday at our staff meeting."

"Thank you. That's all I can ask. If you have any problems, please contact me immediately."

"We will certainly do that." She stands, and I follow her lead. When I return to the office, Tessa is still gone.

"Is she coming back, or have I lost her forever to some pint-sized playboy?" I ask the secretary.

"She's fine. I told her she's welcome to stay the rest of the day if she'd like. That way, she can pick up her books and get her assignments before the weekend. The school is closed tomorrow for teacher in-service."

"Oh. Okay then."

"Just make sure you're in line on the east side by three-thirty to pick her up." And just like that, I'm dismissed. It feels weird to just leave her here without so much as a goodbye. That's how we parted ways the last time. Her mother just disappeared with her without so much as letting me know.

I was just gifted a half day to get some things done. Driving home, my mind reels with everything I still need to do. Childcare. New place. Medical appointments for her. Check next week's shift.

What I do is stumble into my apartment and slump on the couch. I set the alarm on my phone for three-fifteen just in case. I don't want to be late on the first day.

That's the only reason I make it on time to pick Tessa up. Two seconds after my butt hit the couch, I was asleep. I should have run by Eliot's office on the way home. At this point, I'm sure she's given up on me. I shove those thoughts to the back of my brain when Tessa, with a grin from ear to ear, climbs into my cruiser.

"How was your day?" I ask.

"Oh my gosh, Uncle Owen. I got invited to a birthday party. I didn't even know anyone, and just like that, this girl said I should come. And she gave me an invite." She waves a card in my face.

"Colton said she's one of the cool girls. That means I should go, right? What am I going to wear? Anyway, Colton says I'll be a knockout in anything I pick. Colton plays baseball. He thinks I should come to one of his games."

She rambles on about school the entire way to the apartment. All I know by the time we arrive is I've grown to hate Colton. I know, it's stupid. But Tessa is way too young to get mixed up with some player of a seventh grader. I might need to wear my uniform next time I pick her up just to let this boy know where he stands.

Don't judge. I'm just trying to survive.

sixteen

ELIOT

I HAVE TO ADMIT, the views of town are pretty good
from up here. You can see the whole thing from my chair.
The night sky is teaming with stars, and the weather is
perfect.

You can finally fill the nip of fall in the air. And if I get
cold, the fire I started should keep me warm. Even if it's just
a bunch of tiny fires shaped in a D and a C on the hill
behind the football field. It's the same emblem that is on
the front of the letterman jacket that hangs in my closet.

You usually only see this lit up for homecoming, but I
decided to make a random Wednesday night the exception.
When the kids in high school set this thing on fire any time
but on homecoming night, they hightailed it out of here.
It's not like you can't see it from town after all. I'm more
safety-minded though. Don't want to take a chance on
burning up the pasture.

This was a late addition to the list. I overheard some

teenagers talking about homecoming and decided to add it. I should have invited someone to help me. It's kind of lonely up here roasting marshmallows on my own.

As if reading my mind, a sheriff's cruiser pulls up near the fieldhouse. Long, skinny legs swing out of the driver's door. It's not Owen. Not that I was hoping for it to be him or anything.

I watch as the deputy slowly climbs the hillside up to me. "Hey, Eliot," Arlo says a little winded.

"Hey," I respond. "Marshmallow?" I hold out an extra roasting stick and the bag toward him.

He shrugs and takes them. I stare out at the town below as he wrestles with his stick. He finally gets his marshmallow over the fire and slides onto an upturned stump. You can tell where the local teenagers have been; they always leave improvised chairs behind. Makes life convenient.

"So what are you doing up here, Eliot?" Arlo asks.

"Just taking in the view. Eating a snack."

"You know you can't just light the sign whenever, right?" He pops his toasted marshmallow in his mouth. "Jusohomcomin," he says around the gummy mess. I hand him a beer from the cooler next to me. He shrugs again and tips it back. "I said, just on homecoming."

"Show me the amendment to the town charter that says that."

"Eliot," he smirks.

"Fine, it should die down shortly. Another marshmallow?"

"I wish I could, but I just came on shift." He hands me the rest of his beer. "With Owen having to go to days since the kid arrived, we're trading nights. It'll be nice when he's back in the rotation." He stands. "Well, be careful up here and make sure everything is out before you leave. I'll handle calming down Mr. Hamby."

"Thanks, Arlo."

He gives me a small wave and starts down the hill. Another truck pulls up to the fieldhouse. This one I recognize immediately. Reed climbs out and pulls a chair out of the bed. He begins to climb, stopping halfway to visit with Arlo.

When he reaches me, he unfolds his chair and flops down. I hand him a beer and the marshmallow supplies.

"So, no Owen this time, huh?" he asks when he's got his snack over the fire.

"Arlo said he's working days."

"I guess it's pretty hard finding someone to watch the kid."

"Yeah, Brontë stressed out trying to find someone in Austin for Keats when they're working."

"Have you spoken to Owen since that all went down?"

"No. He's sent a couple of texts, but I haven't responded. I'm sure he's busy."

Reed nods before loading his mouth full of food. We sit in silence while he tries to swallow. I don't want to talk about Owen anyway. I'm not sure what to do. He hasn't mentioned cashing in on that raincheck in the few short texts he's sent. I just figure we're better off letting things cool back down between us.

I miss him though. It's hard to admit, but I do. He was warm and funny. He never got angry no matter how far off the rails I went. I think he was even starting to enjoy the chase.

"We've been good friends for a while now," Reed says suddenly.

"Best friends."

"Best friends," he agrees with a grin. It only lasts a second before he grows serious. "Then, can I shoot straight with you?"

"Sure." Why not? I doubt that I'll like what he has to say, but if your best friend can't give you the cold hard facts, who can?

"I've been worried about you for a while." He turns to face me. I don't comment. "You've not been happy." I open my mouth to protest, but he holds up a hand before I can. "Let me finish. I think the old Eliot was starting to make an appearance again. And not old like thirty old." He rolls his eyes. "I mean the Eliot that laughed without apology. The one that helped me win her sister over."

"That Eliot was younger and sprier."

"That was less than a year ago." He grins again.

"This Eliot is now older and grumpier."

"This Eliot," he says, poking me in the ribs. "Has been happier lately than I've seen in a long time. And I think maybe Owen has something to do with that."

I shrug. What do I say? He's right. Not that I need some man to come along and make life worth living, but I was happier when Owen was around.

"Look," Reed continues. "If he's turned into an asshole, then I'll be the first one to tell you to write his ass off. But maybe before you do that, you give him the benefit of the doubt. From what I've heard around town, he's over-whelmed.

"I guess he's asked all over town if anyone is willing to watch a twelve-year-old all night when he has to work the night shift. You know childcare can be hard to find in this town. I was lucky Mel agreed to help with Gram when I needed her."

I give Reed the side-eye. "When did you get to be the wise one?"

"Yes!" He fist pumps toward the sky. "I have waited so long for you to admit I'm smarter than you."

"Umm, I'm sorry, who was valedictorian?"

"You," he says, hanging his head. He knows I'm teasing. I can see the grin still firmly planted on his face.

"And who once peed on an electric fence on a dare?"

"Me," he sighs. "It was transformative. I almost died."

"You didn't almost die; you just wished you had. I rest my case."

"So mean," he whispers.

I laugh. "Come on, help me check that the fires are out." I stand and pull him to his feet. "We should be getting home."

"Yeah. Austen sent me for milk. She's probably wondering what happened." As if on cue, his phone rings. "Hello?" I can hear my sister on the other end. "I was fixing to go get some. I'll be back in a little while."

"You've been in Texas too long," I say, shaking my head. "You're fixing to?"

"It's your sister. She's a bad influence."

"No doubt."

Reed helps me check each can to confirm the fires are completely out. We shake a little sand in them just to be safe. He carries the cooler and his chair behind me down the hill. Good thing I remembered to bring a flashlight. After helping me load my things, he waves and heads for the store.

He's given me a lot to think about. No one wants to hear that they're worried about. I need to step up instead of moping around. There are bound to be things Owen needs help with.

I've been so worried about myself that I forgot about everyone else. Including the one person who needs me. Tomorrow, I need to work on being a better me instead of simply marking something off a list.

* * *

I'll just say it: I'm too old to eat that many marshmallows in one sitting. The fact they all tasted a little like gasoline might be part of why I don't feel so great today.

Then there was the beer. If I have to belch even one more NASCAR firebomb, I might die. That's on top of trying to do the audit for the school system. I've been meaning to get to it for a while. Now, I'm running behind.

"Hi," a chipper voice at my door says. I look up slowly to find the girl from Owen's apartment.

"Hi?"

"I'm Tessa," she says, charging into my office. She drops a backpack that looks as big as she is and plops down in one of my side chairs.

"Eliot."

"I'm supposed to be at the coffee shop doing home-work. Uncle Owen lets me walk there until he's finished with his shift." Wait, what? "But I decided today to find you. Uncle Owen says you're his girlfriend, but I'm not buying that since you haven't come over even once. So I decided to come meet you. You should know it's chill with me if you want to come over."

"Owen's your uncle?" I'm trying to catch up. She talks much faster than I can listen.

"Well, yeah. Who did you think he was?"

"Your dad?"

"Gross. Even someone my age knows you can't marry

your sister. So, do you want to come have dinner with us sometime? Uncle Owen isn't a great cook, but it's edible. We eat a lot of eggs. Like a lot a lot.

"Anyway, Uncle Owen says you're really smart. Do you think I could come get help with math when I need it? I promise I'll only come here when I can't figure it out."

"Sure?"

"Cool. I'd better go before I get in trouble because he can't find me. Oh, do you think you could talk to Uncle Owen about letting me go to the middle school dance with Colton? He's really yummy. Colton, not my uncle. Anyway, I'll see you later. Bye, Eliot." She sweeps out of the office the same way she swept in.

"Bye?"

Her head pops back around the doorframe. "Oh, he really likes you too. You should call him." Poof, she's gone again.

It takes all my concentration not to answer with another question again. What just happened? Maybe those gas-fume marshmallows were deadlier than I thought. I think I'm hallucinating.

I rewind everything trying to piece it together. Why did I never consider that she might be his niece? So did his sister have an emergency that required her to leave Tessa in Owen's care? Or did she just dump the girl and run?

My head hurts. It's only four-thirty, but I'm going home anyway. I can catch a nap before dance lessons this evening.

Packing up my laptop, I head out the door. That's the beauty of owning your own small business. Sure, you work twice as hard, but you can also leave early when you need to. I walk the handful of blocks to my house. I'll just lie down for a half hour. They say that's enough to recharge your batteries.

I'm woken up by the faint sound of my phone ringing in my purse. I didn't even make it to the bed for a nap. I'm face down on the couch. With a yawn, I hunt through my purse for my phone.

"Hello?"

"Where were you? Owen had to dance with Missi," Austen blurts out. "She was on him like he was the last life raft."

"What time is it?" I rub my eyes and stand. Crossing to my living room window, I draw back the curtain to look outside. It's dark out.

"It's eight. You missed dance class."

"Shit. I laid down for a nap. I guess I slept through it."

"Did you know it's his niece living with him, not his daughter? He doesn't have a daughter, or a son, for that matter. I asked when he introduced us to Tessa. She sat on the floor the entire night. She's adorable, Eliot."

"Yeah, I know. I met her earlier today." I'm still struggling with processing what's being said. Moving to my refrigerator, I pull out a bottle of water. Austen's still rambling on about something.

"Hey, I need to get something to eat. Do you think this can wait until later?"

"Fine. But you need to figure your shit out, Eliot. He's not going to wait forever." She hangs up.

How come I'm suddenly the bad guy in this relationship? All I did was take a nap. I remember being the woman scorned when I went to sleep. I check my phone. Yep, same day. Except now I'm being told I'm the bad guy. That was some nap.

This all seems like something that can keep until tomorrow. It's not like I have a leash on him anyway. If he wants to tango with Missi, then that's his right. Doesn't mean I still won't cut that bitch. Oi. I need another nap.

seventeen

ELIOT

"HEY," a chipper voice greets me. "Where were you last week?" I check my watch. I know I agreed to help Tessa with her math if she needs it. I just didn't think that would be today. It's Monday. Even at four in the afternoon, Monday is still rough.

She plops her backpack on the floor and begins digging through it. A math book slaps the corner of my desk.

"Please, settle in." I know... I could be nicer to the girl. But... Monday.

"Thanks, I will," she grins. "So, where were you? I had to sit on the floor for an hour while Uncle Owen got groped by some skank."

"Are you sure you're old enough to know what a skank is?"

"Duh." She rolls her eyes. Great, another smartass. There's only room for one of those in this small office, and I called dibs years ago. "He was just there for you, you know. I mean, I get it. But, listen, I really need you to convince him

147

I'm old enough to go to the dance. You've got to be on my side. Like chicks before dicks."

"Okay. Slow down there, Sailor Mouth." She *is* like me. I have a mini-me. "I agreed to mathematical assistance, not match-making intervention." Or some Venuses before penises grudge match.

"Look. If you're going to be Uncle Owen's girlfriend, you have to be on board for all of it. That includes my baggage."

"Yeah, but I'm not your uncle's girlfriend last time I checked."

"Are you sure about that?" She winks at me.

"Look, I haven't talked to him in two weeks."

"And whose fault is that?"

I open my mouth to respond then close it. Damn if she's not right. I can't just lay all the blame for this relationship going ice-cold solely on Owen.

It's time to have a conversation. The fact he showed up at dance lessons with his niece in tow must mean he agrees. How many times did I tell Austen to sit down with Reed and have a simple conversation? I'm horrible at taking my own advice.

"How about we focus on math right now? I'm sure the rest will work itself out." I clear a space next to me. Tessa scoots her chair around and opens her math book.

"How good at statistics and probability are you?" she asks.

"You are speaking my love language."

Tessa stays half an hour as we work through her home-work. She picks it up fast. Turns out, she's sharp as a tack. I enjoy having her here more than I'd like to admit. She tells me all about the boy in seventh grade she has a crush on. He sounds a lot like Reed at that age. If that's the case, she's a lost cause.

"Do you think I could come back tomorrow?" she asks, packing up her stuff.

"That's fine, but you should probably tell your uncle."

"Nah, he's fine. He'll just give me a lecture about interrupting your workday. But you're cool with me being here, right?" She glances at me. Her eyes show how vulnerable she is. At that moment, it doesn't matter what I have going on. I'll make room for Tessa.

"I'm cool, but you need to start showing up with coffee." I pull a five out of my wallet. "Medium, vanilla latte. Hot."

"You got it, professor." She grins at me. "Tomorrow." Grabbing the five, she gives me a wave over her shoulder as she walks out the door. Something about Tessa makes me think she's twelve going on twenty. I shake my head. I can't wait to see what she throws at me tomorrow.

Tessa shows up the next afternoon and the one after that bearing coffee. We talk about math, boys, seventh grade, and anything else that pops into her brain. I've found myself coming into the office early just so I have the time to devote to her in the afternoon. Today, I hauled a small table upstairs so she has somewhere to work. She still hasn't told Owen.

"Guess what?" she asks, bursting through the door.

"Only four words in the English language end in d-o-u-s."

"What?" She looks at me like I've gone completely mental.

"You said to guess."

"What are they? The words?"

"Horrendous, tremendous, hazardous, stupendous."

"Huh." She stands, still considering that information. Then she shakes her head and hands me my coffee. "Anyway," she draws out. "I totally got busted yesterday. Uncle Owen got off early, and I wasn't at the coffee shop when he showed up."

"How did that work for ya?"

"Look," she says, waving something an inch in front of my face. I lean back until a phone comes into focus. "I got a huge lecture until I told him I was here. He just took me to the phone store and bought me a phone."

"So he's cool with you coming here after school?"

"He's totally cool with it." She's so excited about the phone she's bouncing in front of me. "He said he likes my initiative in finding someone as brilliant as you to tutor me in math. I just needed to let him know next time."

"That sounds like sound advice."

"Right?! He said he'd just wait for me at the station. I don't have to rush back."

"Then I guess we should get to it." She grins and sets her new phone on my desk. I notice a selfie of her and some ridiculously cute boy on the screen saver. "Hold on. Is this the infamous Colton?"

"Isn't he gorgeous?"

"I think I now understand why your uncle is worried," I say. She slumps into a chair. "But I know Colton's parents, and they're nice people. I'll be keeping an eye on this one."

"Not you too." She flaps her arms in frustration. I might be wrong. This kid might be more like Austen. That's fine. I've had years of learning how to deal with drama. "I have an idea. Why don't you come to dinner tonight and let Uncle Owen know his parents are nice? That might help."

"Sorry. I can't tonight. I have something I need to do."

"Is it something crazy that'll get you in trouble with the sheriff? Uncle Owen has told me all about some of the things you've done. Can I come?" I suspect in high school she'll do what I have planned for tonight, but I'm not about to be the person who introduces her to it.

"No, you can't come. It's something I need to do on my own."

"Can you give me a hint for when I'm grilled later for information? Uncle Owen is going to want to know what your plans are. He asks every day when we head home. He thinks he's being all stealthy about it." She laughs. "He's not fooling me. He's so into you."

I smile then I scowl. If he's so into me, why can't he tell me that himself? I ignore her question and pull her math book to me. Negative numbers this time. Gross. I sigh and begin the lesson. At least it will take my mind off of Owen and all the questions I have. Nothing gets your mind off your life like some good old negative numbers.

* * *

OWEN

"What do you mean you don't know what she has planned?"

"I mean she didn't tell me what she's doing." Tessa rolls her eyes. I've gotten a lot of that lately. I also know I'm grilling my twelve-year-old niece about Eliot's plans when I should just call her myself. "She did mumble something about it being a cold jump."

"She's jumping from something?" I yell. She raises an eyebrow at me. "Sorry."

"Colton said that in the summer, everyone goes to the river where there's this cliff you can jump off of. Maybe that's where she's going. He said it's what the high school kids do."

"Then how does he know about it?" No, I haven't warmed up to this Colton kid yet. I get another eye roll. I'll let it drop for now. "What do you want for dinner?"

"Uncle Owen," she draws in frustration. "Just call her."

"I will."

"Soon. Before it's too late."

"I will," I say a little more emphatically. We pull into the driveway.

"Men," she says, rolling her eyes. Pushing her door open, she hops out. "Sometimes you guys are so dense."

"Hey." I follow her up the stairs. "I can still put you in timeout, you know."

"But you won't because you know I'm speaking the truth," she says with a smile.

Yeah, she's right. About calling Eliot, not about being dense. At least, I don't think I'm dense. But I need to talk to Eliot. Tessa is right about that. I pull out my cell phone and call the two people who would know where to find her.

"Hey, man," Reed says when he answers. "Haven't heard from you in a while. How are things going?"

"They're going. I have two favors to ask."

"Shoot."

"I need to know where I can find Eliot. She said something about jumping off some cliff the kids jump off of in the summer."

"Damn, that's going to be a cold jump. I can tell you how to get there."

"Great. Can you and Austen watch Tessa for a little while?"

"No," Austen yells into the phone. "We'll keep her for the night. We can binge on pizza, movies, and smores. It'll be a slumber party."

"You heard the woman," Reed adds. "Bring her on over. What does she eat on her pizza?" I tell him what pizza to order, and he shares how to get to the cliff at the river. Now I just have to get Tessa to agree to stay with Reed and Austen.

"Hey, Tessa," I call after hanging up.

"Yeah?" she asks, walking out of the bedroom.

"How would you like to go to a slumber party at Miss Caraway's house? The librarian."

"Oh my gosh, really?"

She's a lot more excited than I thought she would be.

"Do I really get to hang out with her and her totally lush boy toy?"

"Not if you're going to call him that."

"Oh, Uncle Owen, it's fine. I'll go pack."

I run my hand down my face as she disappears back into the bedroom. If this is only twelve, how am I supposed to survive the teenage years?

I move to the small laundry area and change into jeans and a long-sleeve T-shirt. It's easier if I just leave my clothes folded on the dryer. Getting a turn in the bathroom has become next to impossible. I've got to find somewhere bigger.

When Tessa finally returns to the living room, she's dragging one of my duffels with her. It's only slightly smaller than a steamer trunk. I only use it if I plan on being gone for a week or more.

"Tessa, it's just one night," I remind her.

"You don't know. It could be extended."

"Fine. Let's go." I do know from living with Tessa in the past that you have to pick your battles. Her mother was the same way. If she wants to take half her room with her, that's Austen's problem now. I grab up the deceptively heavy duffle and follow her out. "What are there bricks in this thing?"

She ignores me. It only takes a few minutes to pull up outside Reed's house. Tessa jumps out and flies up the steps to hug Austen. I get out of the car and pull her bag from the trunk.

"I'll get that," Reed says, walking to the cruiser. "Looks like I'll be hiding at The Cougar Den tonight. Brontë and the baby are on the way over."

"Sorry."

"Don't be sorry. Rand and I get a night of freedom." He laughs. "There is something I want to say before you leave though." He grows serious. "Be careful with Eliot. I know she comes across as a badass, but she can still be hurt. This family has relied on her to be the voice of reason for way too long, regardless of how it affects her. It would be nice to see her finally find what makes her happy."

"I have no intention of hurting her. My plan is to beg until she takes me back. I'm just hoping I'm not too late."

Reed smiles and slaps me on the back. He takes the bag from my hands. Without another word, he walks back inside his house.

Now I just have to explain that to Eliot.

OWEN

I'VE NEVER GOTTEN past my heart speeding up to the point of leaping from my ribcage when I see her. This is no exception.

Reed told me I needed to park near the bottom and hike up the hill to reach the cliffs. I did as he instructed, and now I'm slightly winded standing behind her. Not close enough that I'll scare her but so I can watch her hair play in the breeze.

"You know it's impossible for you to sneak up behind me, right?" she says without turning around.

"Why's that?"

"Because the very air changes when you're near." My heart double thuds in my chest. I rub on it to try and calm it down to no avail. It's not mine anymore anyway; it belongs to her.

"Can I sit down?" I ask.

"Last time I heard, my name is not on the abstracts for this property."

I try to hide my smile as I sit next to her with my feet dangling over the edge. We sit in silence looking at the river rolling away while I try to organize my thoughts. There are a million things I want to say to her. A million I should say. But everything feels like a jumbled mess inside my brain, so I do the only thing I can. I just begin.

"My sister, Gwyn, grew up in the same home I did. It was full of love, support, and acceptance. Our parents are good, hard-working people. But Gwyn always had a wild streak. At fourteen, that translated into a drug habit."

"Owen. You don't have to—" she says, turning to face me.

"Yeah, I do."

She quiets but remains facing me.

"The first we knew she was pregnant with Tessa was when they called me from the hospital that she was in labor. She had moved out of my parents' house already. I would see her occasionally hanging out with her shady friends."

Eliot takes my hand and squeezes. My mind immediately settles.

"Gwyn disappeared from the hospital, so I brought Tessa home," I continue. "Actually, I took her to Mom and Dad's where I had help. My sister showed back up right before she turned one and whisked her off. That was the first time she took Tessa without warning. She's done it off and on for the last twelve years.

"The last time she pulled her out of school and disappeared, I knew I needed to start again somewhere new. I couldn't just wait to see if she showed up again. I needed a break from my life."

"That's why you took the job in Dansboro Crossing?" Eliot asks.

"Sheriff Rogers met my dad at some conference. Dad put in a call. I think both of my parents knew I needed to get away. It never occurred to me that Tessa would be dumped on my doorstep a thousand miles from home. But this time, Gwyn isn't taking her again. I've been trying to negotiate the red tape to legally adopt her, so she has a steady home from now on."

"Do you think they'll approve the adoption?"

"I'm hopeful. But that's not what worries me. What worries me is that, by not including you in everything that's been happening, I might have lost you." I turn my body so I'm facing her. Taking her other hand, I go for broke.

"Eliot, I'm sorry. I never meant to shut you out. I'm an idiot, but I hope you can look past that because I've fallen in love with you. The idea that I screwed up enough to drive you away is eating me up inside."

"You love me?" she asks, gazing back at me with her warm, whiskey-colored eyes.

"I do. I think it happened when I wasn't paying attention. It just kind of snuck up on me. I'm glad it did though. I can't think of any other woman I'd rather be with than you. Do you think I still have a shot?"

"Hmm," she says, tapping her chin. "Let me think. Do I really want to be with a man who is sexier than his name suggests, goes above and beyond to care for his family, *and* professes his adoration in one of the most romantic settings in this county?"

"Owen's a sexy name. Grandpa was a total sex machine." I smile. Of course, she's being her sassy self. It's my first indication I might be forgiven.

"No," she says, placing a hand over my mouth. "No one's grandpa is a sex machine. But, Owen, you never lost me. I never went anywhere, and I know you've been drowning. I'm pissed at myself for not helping you. I guess we're both just trying to figure out where we go from here."

"Just taking the time to let Tessa invade your work has been huge. For both of us. Do you think you can handle being with someone with so much baggage?"

"Are you kidding? The baggage is the best part." She smirks before pressing her lips to mine.

How did I spend so much time away from her? Why? I should have dragged her out of the Jeep covered in mud to spend the evening with us. I should have shown up the next day just to let her know she's important in my life.

"By the way," she says, leaning back. "I've been in love with you, whether I want to admit it or not, from the first dance."

"Yeah?"

"Yeah." She presses her lips to mine again. When we pull back, she has the most beautiful smile. One I put there. It makes me feel ten feet tall.

"So, are you planning to jump?"

"Maybe."

"Because you don't have to. You don't have to prove anything to anyone. You never have." She raises an eyebrow like she doesn't believe me. "Maybe the reason you didn't do all of this in high school is because you didn't need to. You didn't need to prove to anyone who you were; you already knew. I think they did too. Your self-confidence is the sexiest thing about you. And that's saying a lot because I'm obsessed with your body."

"You know when we get back to civilization, I'm riding you like there's no tomorrow, right?"

"Then let's get this done," I say. Standing, I pull her up next to me. I pull my T-shirt over my head. It's cold but bearable. "Come on, woman. Strip."

She laughs and begins peeling off her clothes.

"Seems like we do a lot of things naked," she says when we're standing on the edge of the rock looking down at the river.

"Not near enough, in my opinion." I grin when she blushes. "On three?"

"Hang on." She takes several deep breaths and grabs my hand. "On three."

"One. Two. Three," we count together. Then we jump. For a moment, we're in free fall. Then I'm underwater. The water is cold. My head breaks the surface, and I look for Eliot.

"It's freezing," she squeals. I swim over and wrap her in my arms. She wraps her legs around my waist.

"You know," I say, slowly swimming us toward the riverbank. "Your sisters kidnapped Tessa for the night."

"I hope you realize she's going to come back neurotic."

"It's a chance I'm willing to take to have a night alone with you."

"Deputy Steele, you're just saying all the right things tonight."

"I have a couple of weeks to make up for." We reach the bank. "Are you ready?"

"No, but let's go." We rush out of the water and head back up the hill to our clothes. It would have been nice if either one of us had thought this out better. Like leaving towels on the bank at the very least. But, nope. We have to streak to our clothes. Shivering, we struggle to redress. At least we mostly dried off on the way back up.

"We could stop for coffee somewhere," I suggest. "And food." She scrunches her face at me. "I promise I'll work it off of you later."

"Well, in that case, how can I refuse?"

We stop at the diner in town. I guess this is the first time we've really been out as a couple. I don't think the pancake supper counts. It would explain the conspiratorial looks and whispering the handful of locals are doing. Eliot acts oblivious as she sips her coffee. Good. Because I plan on a lot of this happening in the future.

"Your place or mine?" she asks.

"Can we go to yours? I moved Tessa into the bedroom at mine."

"Where are you sleeping?"

"On the couch for now. I'm hunting for someplace bigger, but finding rentals here is hard."

"Hmm." Her eyebrows scrunch together, and I wonder what she's thinking. She pops another nacho in her mouth. I can almost see the gears of her mind grinding as she slowly chews. She swallows and tosses her napkin on the table. "Ready?"

"Whenever you are." I walk to the counter to pay. She waits with me. Taking my hand, we walk out together. That should give the local gossips something to talk about.

"I'll follow you," I say, leading her to her car. I'm not prepared when she presses me against it and pulls me down for a kiss. One that sizzles through my veins. This is going to be a long drive.

"Do you really love me?" she asks when she pulls back.

"I do. I really love you."

"Okay. I'll see you at home." She pushes me out of the way and opens her door. I shake my head. Whatever she's got circulating through that beautiful mind promises to be a doozie. I can't wait to find out.

She barely gets the door unlocked at her house before I'm on her. I slam her door closed and lock it. Turning to her, I catch her before she can make it into the living room. Her eyes are the size of saucers, but there's a twinkle of mischief in them. I pull her against me and lift her to my waist. She wraps her legs around me.

Her hands wrestle my shirt over my head. "Slow down," I mumble against her neck. "We have all night."

"And we can go slow on rounds two and three. Right now, I want you inside me." I do like the sound of that.

Setting her back on her feet, I fish my wallet out of my jeans. She watches me pull a condom out. Suddenly, she's spurred into action. Her shirt comes off in one swift tug. Then her pants follow. Within seconds, she's standing against the wall completely nude.

She arches an eyebrow at me. My hands race to unhook my belt and shove my pants to the floor. I don't try to take off anymore before shoving my underwear down and sliding the condom over my throbbing erection. Picking her back up, I ease her heat down my shaft. We both moan.

"It's been too long," she says. It has; way too long. I should be making love to this amazing woman every day. I begin to thrust hard into her. "You know I'm not going to last long, right?" she adds. Jesus. I didn't think it was possible to grow harder, but I do. "Yes, like that." She grinds against my lower abdomen with every thrust.

My hands are clamped firmly to her ass, encouraging her to ride me as hard as possible. I still have use of my tongue though. Tracing a path up her neck, I capture her mouth with mine as she screams through her orgasm.

Lightning shoots up my spine as my body races to join hers. She's pressed so hard against the wall by my spasming body that I don't know how she's still breathing.

"I think you should move in here," she whispers in my

ear. I know I'm trying to recover, but I didn't realize hearing hallucinations were part of orgasms. "You and Tessa."

"You don't get to make crazy comments like that when I'm still inside you," I answer.

"It's not crazy. I've been thinking about this."

"Eliot," I warn. She has no idea what she's proposing.

"No, wait. Let me down," she says, shoving at my shoulders. I set her back on her feet. "Hear me out." She walks toward her bedroom with me following on her heels. "You're not going to find anything. People own their house until they die then someone else buys them. It's rare to rent out a house."

"I'm starting to realize this." We finish in the bathroom and flop on her bed. She props her head on her hands on top of my chest.

"I have three bedrooms, which is plenty of room for both of you. Tessa would still have her own room."

I open my mouth to protest again, but she cuts me off.

"I'm also here every night, which means you don't have to worry about childcare. And she can come to my office after school. Even if we're both busy, I have an entire family that would be happy to help out."

"You're serious." I can't wrap my head around her wanting to do this. "That's a lot to put on yourself, not to mention dragging your family into it."

"Actually, hanging out with Tessa sounds like a great way to spend an evening. She reminds me of my sisters at that age. I miss that." She smiles at me. "I guess you can be underfoot too."

"Let me think about it?"

"Okay." She nods. "Think about it while I suck this dick dry."

I'm moving in. I can already tell as she works her way down my body. There's no way I can say no when her lips wrap around me. It's crazy and it's reckless, but people have done worse. Besides, I can't think of anything better than being a part of the complicated world that's Eliot Caraway.

nineteen

ELIOT

MY PARENTS SHOULD HAVE JUST NAMED me Impulsive. It's what I've become. I didn't really think about moving Owen and Tessa in here before bringing it up. It made sense in my head at the time.

Owen didn't come around easily either. You would think the blow job, doggy style in the shower, cowgirl at midnight, and kitchen island sex while trying to make breakfast would have convinced him.

What convinced him to move them in was when he showed up at eight in the evening two nights later with Tessa in tow to beg me to watch her while he filled in for Ray who was sick.

I make a pretty impressive surrogate parent. She was in bed by ten, lights out at eleven. I managed to get her to school the next morning both clothed and fed. Being the oldest sister prepared me well.

Now, I'm watching Owen haul boxes into my house wondering if I've lost my ever-loving mind. When did I turn into the type of person who moves her boyfriend in after only knowing him for a few months? It's way too impulsive for me. I'm a planner, an organizer. This is the opposite of that in every way.

"I promise this is all of them," Owen says, hauling the last box into the guest room. I know most of his stuff is in a storage unit. The apartment came furnished, so he didn't have to store any of the furniture except a few bookcases. He keeps assuring me that this is temporary until he can find something. I'm not so sure I want it to be temporary.

"Can I call you Aunt Eliot yet?" Tessa says, bounding into the house with a suitcase.

"Umm, okay."

"Rand said it was okay to call him Uncle Rand. He's agreed to help paint my room if you say it's cool. He's so dope. I don't know how your sisters got such gorgeous boyfriends and you're stuck with Uncle Owen."

"I heard that," Owen yells from the other room.

"Whatever," she says, rolling her eyes. "Anyway, do you think I can paint my room?"

"It's your room; you can do what you want with it," I answer.

"What did I say, Tessa?" Owen asks, walking back into the living room.

"That we're probably not staying long. Blah, blah, blah," she mopes. Owen leaves to check the truck one more time, so Tessa leans over to whisper. "He totally wants to stay. I think this is our forever home." I cough to hide my laughter. "I've got the most epic color picked out. It's going to look like a sunset all the time." Well, that should be interesting.

"Tessa, stop bugging Eliot and go unpack your suitcases," Owen says, walking back inside. He doesn't stop until he's wrapped me in his arms. "I'd like to say it gets better. But sometimes I think the talking will never stop." I do laugh this time against his chest.

"She is delightful and you know it. Just wait until she's giving us the silent treatment."

"Now that sounds delightful." I push out of his arms to smack him on the chest.

"Do you think we're crazy for doing this?" I ask.

"I know we are. Who would want to live with a grumpy man and his chatterbox of a niece?" I scowl at him. "Fine. I don't know. I don't know how this will go. It could be the best thing we've ever done or a complete dumpster fire. But there's no way to know without stepping out there. Just like the cliff at the river. Sometimes you just have to jump."

"You're like Yoda. Has there always been this wealth of insight locked in that head of yours?"

"Patience you must have, my young Padawan." His Yoda voice is pretty spot on. That gives me an idea for Halloween next year.

"Can we get pizza tonight?" Tessa asks, bounding down the hallway.

"Actually." I bat my eyes at Owen. He raises an eyebrow in anticipation. I think he gets an adrenaline rush working through my list. Sad, this isn't one of those times. "Tonight's family dinner night, and I sort of said we'd all be there." I mouth the word sorry at him. He just shrugs.

"Oh, my gosh!" Tessa gushes. "Is everyone going to be there?"

"I'm pretty sure."

"I have to let my friends know. They're so jealous that I get to spend so much time with Reed and Rand. They're on the S.H.O.G.L. list at school."

"S.H.O.G.L.?" Owen asks.

"Yeah, smoking-hot old guy list," she says like we're morons who should have known. "You're on it too. Which is gross by the way. Oh, I've got to pick out what I'm going to wear." We stare at her like deer in the headlights as she bounces back down to her room.

"Well," I say when she disappears. "You're definitely on my S.H.O.G.L."

"What the hell?" He runs his hand down his face. "Why couldn't my sister have a boy? Boys I can handle."

"Bruh," I say, slouching. "I don't know where the porn stash under my bed came from."

He laughs. "Point taken."

"Speaking of boys, I'm supposed to convince you to let her go to the seventh-grade dance with Colton."

"Not happening," he responds.

Hmm. We'll see. I went to the seventh-grade dance. Nothing exciting happens. We can always volunteer as chaperones. Wait, what am I saying? I don't want to be trapped at the seventh-grade dance all night. Crap. I've turned myself into the unsuspecting parent of an almost teenager.

"What if I make Austen and Reed go as chaperones?" They need to get out of the house more. I'm sure I can con them into going.

"Do they normally go to the middle school dances?"

"No, but I'm sure I can convince them."

He grins at me. "You are so wily. It's sexy." He pulls me into a kiss.

"Gross" breaks us apart. "No PDA around the minor."

"If you can't handle an occasional display of affection between us," Owen responds, "you can stay in your room."

He grabs me by the front of my shirt and pulls me into an incendiary-inducing kiss. His tongue sweeps across mine once, forcing a moan from my lips before he pulls back. I sway just a little. Damn, the man can kiss.

"Adults!" Tessa exclaims with a shake of her head, but I catch her smile. "Can't live with them; can't go anywhere without one of them driving."

I laugh. I mean, how can you not? The girl is hilarious. Maybe this surrogate mom thing won't be so bad.

"Can we go?"

"Yes, we can go. Just let me throw on a clean shirt." And maybe dry panties. I quickly change, apply fresh deodorant, and run my hairbrush through my tangled hair. Walking back into the living room, I find Owen's done the same.

"Where are we going?" he asks, standing from the couch.

"It's at Rand and Brontë's tonight."

My youngest sister's house is something right out of a magazine. Rand bought it when he decided to settle here permanently. It was a worn-out old Craftsman that he carefully restored to its former self. Only better. I open their front door to find my nephew crawling toward me.

"Come here, you," Owen says, swooping the baby into his arms.

"Oh thank God," Brontë says, stepping out of the kitchen. "He's getting so fast that he's hard to keep up with. One minute, he's right there. The next, he's heading out on his own."

I would expect her to take the baby, but she doesn't. She just returns to the kitchen. Makes sense. Owen touched it. It's his problem now.

"What do you need help with?" I ask.

"Salad." She points the knife she's using to slice a giant ham at the vegetables on the island.

Owen walks in a few minutes later and sidles up behind

me. Wrapping an arm around my waist, he leans over to steal a carrot. His lips brush my temple as he stands back up. It feels nice to finally be the sister with a man pressed against her back. Weird. But nice.

"Where's the baby?" Brontë asks, smiling at us.

"Tessa took him upstairs to play in the nursery until dinner," Owen answers.

"Really? She's a keeper."

"Yeah, she has her moments. Where's Rand?"

"I sent him for ice," she says, a little flustered. "You'd think I could remember something as basic as ice at the store." The front door opens, and I can hear my mother talking loudly to Austen. "Christ, they're already here. Where in the hell is Rand with the ice?"

"Right here, honey," Rand says, walking into the kitchen from the mudroom. He sets two bags in the sink. "I'll go entertain your parents while you finish." He kisses her on the temple just like Owen kissed me. It makes me smile. I'm now the recipient of temple kisses.

"I'll help," Owen says and follows Rand out.

"Tell us all about domestic life with the deputy," Austen says, walking into the kitchen.

"They just moved in today. Hard to do anything too salacious in that time period with a twelve-year-old around," I answer.

"Are you freaked about it yet?" Brontë asks.

"A little bit, yeah." I set the knife down on the cutting board to meet my sisters' gazes. "I think I might have reacted to the heat of the moment before thinking it through."

"Heat of the moment," my sisters say simultaneously with grins. What idiots.

"Seriously though, I think it's great," Austen adds.

"How so?" I want to know because I'm still of the opinion that I've lost my mind.

"I just think he's a good guy that makes you happy. It will be hard for you to get too grumpy with a bubbly almost teenager in the house, and it's nice to have something warm to cuddle up with at night."

"I'm not grumpy." They look at me like I'm a moron.

"Of course not, sweetie." I flip Austen off. She laughs.

I finish chopping up the salad. Tossing the ingredients into a bowl, I leave to put it on the table. Owen is visiting with my parents near the fireplace. He smiles at me.

Setting the salad on the table, I move toward him. He pulls me against his side like we've been together for years. It feels a little awkward but nice at the same time. I guess I should get used to it. I don't think Owen is the type of man to keep this relationship private. That's a nice feeling also.

"Your mom and I are discussing books," he says.

"I have never known her to turn that conversation down. Did y'all put Dad to sleep?"

"Rand made him a whiskey sour," Mom answered. "He's fine." Dad raises his glass in salute.

"Let's eat," Brontë announces, carrying some sort of casserole to the table. "Tessa," she yells.

"Coming," is yelled back from upstairs. Tessa appears with Keats on her hip a few minutes later. "I gave him a fresh diaper," she adds, handing him off to Brontë. "I'm a pretty good babysitter."

"That is information I can use," Brontë answers. "Everyone find a seat." I sit next to Owen. Tessa manages to wiggle between Rand and Reed. I get it. I'd choose the S.H.O.G.L. guys too.

"So, how are you liking your new school?" Dad asks Tessa when we start passing the food around.

"It's good. I have a couple of friends that let me hang out. I even got invited to a birthday party on the first day. Colton said I'm already popular. I've never been popular before. I was told I should try out for cheerleading next year, which would be cool. I can do that and still play basketball. Colton says we have to ride a bus to games."

"Is this Colton Campbell?" Austen asks when Tessa pauses to breathe.

"Yeah. He's been so cool showing me around."

"He's a distant cousin," Reed pipes up.

I stifle a laugh when Owen growls softly. Talking him into letting Tessa go to the dance with Colton is going to be harder than I thought. As far as I've heard, Colton has been nothing but nice to Tessa.

It's hard to explain that to a papa bear though. I know his sister had Tessa when she was young and he's just trying to make sure Tessa chooses a different path, but I don't think he has to worry. I think Tessa is far from following that road.

"Do you think you'll be able to survive living with Eliot?" Dad asks, changing the subject.

"I think so. Time will tell, right? I mean, Uncle Owen put his stuff in the guest room, but I'm not a kid anymore. I know he'll be sneaking over to Eliot's room once he thinks I'm asleep. You can just look at them to tell they're in love."

Owen places his hands over his face. Reed and Rand are both shaking with silent laughter.

"But I'll pretend I don't hear anything."

"Tessa!" Owen barks. "That's enough."

"Oh." She looks down at her plate. "Sorry."

"No, no," Reed laughs. "We want to hear all about it." Austen smacks him in the chest. And they call me the grumpy one.

"Tessa," Dad says. She looks up at him. "Between that one sneaking in my daughter's window at night and that one getting my daughter pregnant, what Eliot and Owen do are the least of our problems. But you can always stay with us if you need a break." She smiles brilliantly at him. So do I.

"In my defense, I married her," Rand says.

Dad snorts, and everyone laughs. Owen's body bangs against mine. He is grinning, and I can't help but think moving them in might have been my best idea yet.

twenty

OWEN

TESSA ISN'T WRONG. I'm absolutely sneaking into Eliot's room after my niece is in bed. Screw it, I'm going in now. Slipping past Tessa's new room, I quietly open the door to Eliot's room, finding her flat on her back on the bed.

"Why is my family so exhausting?" she asks, staring at the ceiling.

"Because they want to know everything that's happening in your life," I say, lying next to her. She slides her body over just enough for me to fit. "That's not a bad thing." I wrap an arm over her, pulling her closer.

"Yeah, I know. They just wear me out."

"Completely out?" I ask, placing a lingering kiss on her neck.

"Mmm, maybe not completely." Moving down, I suck gently on the place where her neck meets her shoulder. She moans. "Yeah, I think completely is too strong a word." Sliding her shirt over her head, I place light kisses on the soft skin above her bra.

"Can you think of a better word?" I ask. My tongue snakes along her rib cage.

"Totally energized." I release her bra strap, freeing her gorgeous breasts. Pulling one of her taut nipples between my lips, I feel her arch up to me.

"I like that better," I say, moving to the other breast. I nip around the sensitive bud.

"Owen," she begs. I smile against her skin as my lips brush over her abdomen. That is my favorite sound in the world now. Hearing Eliot moan my name fills me with a need I can't fight to show her just how much I've fallen in love with her.

My fingers unbutton her pants and pull them down as I ease off the end of the bed. On my knees before her is exactly where I should be. I want to worship every inch of her lush body.

My nose slides along her panties, breathing in her scent. Sliding my hands into the waistband, I add them to the growing pile of clothes on the floor. Then I get to work.

"Owen," she cries as my tongue glides through her folds.

It won't take me long to make her come like this. It hasn't before anyway. I flick her clit with my tongue. I'm rewarded with a gasp. She begins to grind against me when I press it inside her.

My thumb takes over working her clit as I fuck her with my tongue. It doesn't take much to have her stiffen under me in orgasm. The way she desperately clenches around my tongue almost has me coming apart also, but I want to hold out until I'm buried deep inside her.

As she comes down, I stand at the end of the bed. I undress as quickly as possible and begin to hunt in my wallet for a condom.

"You don't need it," she says. I look up at her. Did I hear correctly? "My birth control has kicked in. Hurry." She doesn't have to tell me twice. Pushing her thighs wide, I climb between them.

"Sure?" She nods, and I press inside. It's unlike anything I've experienced before. Condoms are fine, but to feel Eliot's velvety softness with nothing between us is heaven.

My hips rock as I try a test thrust. So. Fucking. Good. I rock against her as she lifts to meet me. Pulling her up onto my thighs, I double my efforts.

"Yes, like that," she pants. "Don't stop." She doesn't have to worry about that. I don't ever want to stop. Not even when we're old and gray. "Owen," she screams. I let her pull me along with her in her climax. I wonder vaguely if we'll ever get slower at this. I doubt it; she turns me on too much to go slow.

"Shit. Do you think Tessa heard us?" she gasps. I laugh. Not the sexiest thing I've heard after sex.

"That's why I bought her noise-reducing headphones to listen to her music with," I answer.

"Sorry. That wasn't sexy at all." Eliot laughs. My cock jerks inside her as she wiggles. If I don't climb off now, neither one of us is getting any sleep tonight. I roll over on the bed to stare at the ceiling.

"Oh, I don't know. It sounded perfect to me. Very Eliot-like."

"Is that good or bad?" She rolls on her side until she's sprawled on my chest. My hand begins making slow circles on her back.

"I hope you never change. I love you just the way you are."

"Stop it," she scolds, lightly slapping my chest. "It'll piss me off if you make me cry."

I laugh. It would have been impossible for me to pick out a woman meant for me more than Eliot. The humor most people call acerbic, I find funny. I've finally learned that all of the messes she's been getting into aren't a plea for attention. It's just Eliot being Eliot.

"Did you get everything crossed off your list?"

"Almost. There are two left."

"Let's hear it."

"I'm not sure you'll be okay with one."

My hand slides down to her ass. "Then maybe you had better convince me."

"I'd be more than happy to try." With a wicked grin, she swings her leg over me. She straddles my hips and grinds against my growing erection.

"Fine," I moan. "I'm onboard."

* * *

I should have my head examined. Damn her sexy body for convincing me to do this. It's my first day off since she talked me into this. Tessa is spending the day with one of her friends. Having a girlfriend with a sister as the local librarian is priceless when it comes to Tessa's friends. She knows who I can trust Tessa to without running background checks on their parents.

Eliot insisted I wear all black for what she has planned. I've tried pointing out that it's still daylight outside, but she ignored me. So because I agreed to go along, I'm wearing black jeans, a black long-sleeved T-shirt, and black boots.

"Don't forget, you're aiming for Reed," she whispers. I'm not sure why she's whispering. Reed and Austen are nowhere in sight. But she's assured me that it's date night, which is why I'm hunkered down behind her car in the parking lot of Sam's Steak Shack. My knees are starting to ache.

"I don't understand what we're doing exactly," I admit.

"During senior week, the freshmen have a day they get to chalk bomb the seniors at the end of class. I was sick my freshman year, so I didn't get to bomb anyone. Then my senior year, I was away at the U.I.L. state calculus competition, so I didn't get bombed."

"You competed in math at state?"

"I didn't just compete. I won," she answers.

"So damn sexy."

She blushes for a moment before grabbing my arm. "There they are. Ready?" Probably not, but I nod. I'm not altogether positive this isn't assault. "Now."

We raise up and lob our chalk bombs at her sister and her fiancé. My bomb hits Reed square in the chest, exploding pink chalk all over the front of him. Austen gets hit in the side. She is covered in green chalk.

"Damn it, Eliot," Reed yells. She's already grabbed my hand, and we're running down a side street. I can't stop laughing. Neither can she. When we're certain Reed isn't chasing us down, we slide to a stop.

"Oh, my god, that was awesome," she says. "Let me see where Brontë is." She pulls out her phone and checks the friends' app. "This says they're at home. Come on."

I have the bucket of bombs, so we decide to leave Eliot's car in the parking lot and walk. She makes me wait down the block while she does reconnaissance.

Hopefully, no one looks out their front windows. Standing aimlessly dressed in black is certain to send off warning bells. At least it's starting to grow dark. It's not long before she comes stalking back to me.

"They're in the backyard. We can cut through the neighbor's yard to surprise them."

"The neighbors won't mind?"

"She's like a hundred and twenty years old. She won't notice." I shake my head but follow her anyway. Of course, I do. We walk around the block and cut through a side yard. There's no fence, which helps our trespassing. Unfortunately, Rand put in a tall privacy fence when he had the pool put in.

"Climb on my shoulders," I whisper, squatting down. Eliot looks at me like I've lost my mind. "Come on." When she's sitting squarely on my shoulders, I raise slowly so she can see into the yard.

"They're sitting by the fire pit," she whispers.

"Where's the baby?"

"Must already be asleep because he's not out here."

"Good. Here." I hand one of the bombs from the bucket to her. "Take two. You'll have to fire fast so we can run." I place another bomb in her hand. I feel it when she pulls her arm back and lets the first one fly. I also hear Brontë squeal when the first one hits her. Rand just grunts when she hits him.

"Eliot! You're done," Brontë yells as I lower Eliot back to the ground. We're laughing so hard this time that it's hard for us to stagger out of the neighbor's yard.

"That was even better than Reed and Austen," she says as we walk back toward her car. I only agreed to this if we kept it in the family.

"You know they're already planning retribution, right?"

"Pssh. Bring it." We slow our pace to a leisurely stroll. "I can't believe you agreed to this." She's holding my hand.

"I can't believe I did either. I'm pretty sure there's

nothing in the law enforcement manual about helping a citizen chalk bomb their siblings."

I wouldn't change tonight for the world though. I don't care how much trouble we get in. I'm so madly in love with Eliot I would do anything she asks. I didn't realize when I moved to this sleepy little town that I could find such happiness simply holding hands on the sidewalk.

"How many bombs do we have left?"

"Three maybe," I say, digging through the bucket.

"Perfect. I have one more target."

"It's not your parents, is it? I don't think I'll ever get in good with your dad if I hurl a chalk bomb at him."

"Please, my dad thinks you're the best thing since sliced bread. But no, we won't be hitting my parents. Even I don't have that big of a death wish. Nope, I have someone else in mind."

She pulls me through town until we're standing at the back parking lot door of the bar I hauled her off the table at. Shoving me behind the nearest car, she pulls out her phone. I guess my biggest question is, why does she have the phone number for the bar memorized? Before I can ask, she slides the phone back into my pocket and grabs a bomb in each hand.

"This is for ratting me out," she yells at Kevin when he steps outside. He takes the bombs hitting him square in the chest like a man. I'm more than a little impressed.

"Come on, Eliot," he yells.

"You owed me, Kevin."

"Fair enough," he agrees, shaking his head. "Y'all want to come in for a beer?"

"Absolutely." She unloads the last bomb at him. He takes that one too before holding the door for us. I shake his hand on the way by and shrug. What can I do? Eliot has a mind of her own. I've learned there's not a lot I can do to change it. I think Kevin understands. She leads me to a table.

"What do you have against Kevin?" I ask. I'll have to buy him a beer (or six) at some point.

"Nothing. He's just fun to jack with. I do the bar's taxes, so he knows I'll give him a discount at tax season," she answers. "It's a pretty good trade-off for a little chalk in your hair."

"This seems like a drink to match your personality," Kevin says, setting a green drink in front of her. "My take on a Pain in the Ass." He sets a beer in front of me. Smirking, he walks back to the bar.

"Don't forget the cheese fries," she yells after him. "See, it's all just in fun."

"Just in fun, huh?"

"Yeah, much like later when you put those handcuffs to good use."

"Drink faster," I demand, holding up her glass.

She laughs before taking a big swallow. I can't believe I'm this lucky.

twenty-one

ELIOT

"I'VE GOT to get Tessa to school." I ease my eyes open to find Owen, fully dressed, standing in the bedroom.

"At seven in the morning?" I think that's what my clock says. "On a Saturday?"

"She has a school trip, remember."

"On a Saturday?"

"Yes," he answers, bending over to kiss my forehead. "On a Saturday. I'm going straight to work from there, so I'll see you later."

He flies out of the bedroom before I can answer. The front door slams closed, and the house falls quiet again.

Weird. I thought Owen took the day off for my birthday. Yep, you heard right. Today is D-day. That dreaded f, dash, dash, dash birthday. The big three-oh. And I've been abandoned to my own devices for the day.

Staring up at the ceiling, I replay the conversation. He didn't even wish me a happy birthday. No breakfast in bed. No birthday song. Not even any spankings. Maybe he's planning on breaking up with me later. That would make it a banner day. I might as well spend the day learning to cackle and collecting cats.

Throwing off the duvet, I listen to my ankles creak when I stand. Sounds about right. At least the shower lets me stand inside its hot spray while I wallow in self-pity as long as I want. I dress as I try to decide what to do with myself today. Austen and Brontë are taking me to lunch at least.

I wander into the kitchen, jonesing for some coffee. Sitting on the counter is a cinnamon roll. One of those big jobs with raisins and nuts in it. It sits on a dinner plate with a candle stuck in the middle. A note lays in front of it with the words: *I bet you thought I forgot. Happy birthday. Be dressed to go out when I get home tonight. Dress warm. Love, Owen.*

Okay, he's redeemed himself a little. Surely he wouldn't make me dress up for a breakup. It's a little cryptic though. Dress warm? Like we're going ice skating in Norway warm or the movie might be a little chilly warm? I shrug, turning to the coffee maker. There's a cup warming for me. Inside the refrigerator is a fresh carton of cream. Owen was a busy boy this morning.

Pouring coffee into the largest cup I can find, I flop onto the couch, fork in hand. I have to fit into the tiny hole left by the middle school student turned junior jock. There's a softball glove, basketball, sweatshirt, pair of cleats, and an opened backpack covering the remaining area. I'm going to have to get something for the garage that can hold all of this before we die under a teenage girl hoard.

What should I do with myself? Somehow spending the day on the couch watching television seems wrong. Plus, it now smells like the perfume counter at Sephora. There's only one more item on my list, and I can't do it alone. I guess I could go to the office. It should be quiet so I can catch up on some work.

Returning to the bedroom, I pull on a pair of jeans and a flannel. My image in the mirror looks less fashion catalog and more serial killer. Seems about right.

The walk to my office is uneventful. No clowns with balloons jump out. Thankfully. No strippers with a boombox. Sadly. Not even a drive-by birthday mooning from Reed. And yes, he did that for my eighteenth.

The office is equally quiet. With a sigh, I fire up my computer. Accounting doesn't wait for your birthday festivities to end. I should be able to get a few hours in before meeting my sisters for lunch. At least finish up the school audit.

"What the hell are you doing?" I jump at Brontë's voice. Looking at the clock on the wall, I see it's past when I was supposed to meet them. You know the saying. Time flies when you're doing math. Or something like that.

"Sorry. I lost track of time," I say, shutting down my computer.

"No, I mean what are you doing at your office at all? And why aren't you answering your phone?" she asks.

"I forgot to turn the do-not-disturb off," I mumble, checking the infernal thing on my desk.

"Come on, we're late."

"Where are we going?"

"We have appointments at Nailed Her for mani/pedis. Lunch has already been delivered."

Brontë snaps her fingers and points down the hall. I guess that's supposed to speed me up? The computer only shuts down so fast. I would prefer not to lose a morning's worth of work. Grabbing my purse, I chase after her. She can really turn on the runway stride when she wants.

She's already in her car when I reach the parking lot. It's one of Rand's sports cars. He is one brother-in-law with some nice perks.

Brontë revs the car, and we squeal out of the parking lot. In what feels like 2.3 seconds, we arrive at Nailed Her, also known as Lynn's to the locals. I follow Brontë inside only to find the place completely void of old ladies getting ready for church on Sunday.

"What happened here?" I ask in astonishment. I can't remember a Saturday without the place brimming with octogenarians.

"We rented the whole place so you could have a day of being pampered," Austen answers, crossing the room to kiss me on the cheek. "No one around to comment on your cohabitation with the deputy. Happy birthday." I debate bursting into tears for a moment, but that's not my style. Still, this is pretty awesome.

"Come on, sweetheart," Lynn says, waving me toward her. "I've got a seat with your name on it."

I walk to the pedicure chair. Taking off my shoes and socks, I climb into the seat. My feet ease into the bubbling water. A plate with a fancy sandwich is thrust into my hands. Ahhh. This is the life.

"Speaking of cohabitation," Austen begins. "How is living with Owen going?"

"It's good. His shifts are erratic, so that took some getting used to. But, good." I can't think of another word to describe nights of earth-shattering orgasms, days of working on the house together, and meals cooked as a family filled with laughter. It really is... good.

"Has the teenage drama started yet?" she asks.

"Not too bad. She's working hard on Owen to let her go to the seventh-grade dance with this Colton kid. So far, Owen refuses to even talk about it."

"How bad can it be?" Brontë asks. "I remember the seventh-grade dance being pretty tame. What has this boy got that has his hackles up?"

"Do you remember Reed when he first moved to town?"

"That cute, huh? Yeah, that's bad," she agrees. "Still, I think he should let her go."

"I agree, but I can't get into the middle of it."

"Why?" Austen says. "You're the only one in town he'll listen to."

"What color, honey?" Bless Lynn for saving me from any more of this conversation.

"She needs something that says she puts out hard for a certain live-in sheriff's deputy," Brontë pipes up. "But she's no slut."

"I'm not sure I have that one," Lynn says, looking through her polish. "How about Sultry in the Sack red instead?"

"Perfect," my sisters agree.

The next hour passes in bliss. I get caught up on all the local gossip while eating my sandwich, which turns out to be three tiny sandwiches. It's the first time I've tried watercress, whatever that is. Dessert is a small box of cupcakes I choose from. It's not that hard to decide. I mean, who doesn't snatch up the chocolate one?

By the time we're done, I have red toes and fingers. It's a little over the top for me, but fuck it, it's my damn birthday. Brontë returns me home with threats to my person if I go back to the office. I wave from the door and walk into my house. It's still just as quiet as this morning. What am I supposed to do with myself until tonight?

Inspiration hits me when I walk into the bedroom. Stripping to my shirt, I crawl between the sheets. A nap is always a good idea. I don't remember falling asleep, but I'm woken by a pair of lips pressed against my temple. My eyes flit open to find a very handsome man looking down at me.

"Hey, gorgeous," Owen says.

"What time is it?" I moan, sitting up. The clock beside the bed says six. "Shit, I'm supposed to be ready to go out." I bound up from the bed and sway as my equilibrium fights to catch up. Owen's strong arms wrap around me.

"Slow down. We're not on any time crunch," he says.

I try to push out of his arms to head for the closet anyway, but he's looking down at my flame-red toes. Without turning me loose, his gaze lands on the clock. Then he looks back down at my feet. He considers me for a full minute before shaking his head.

"I'll revisit that later," he growls.

My lady bits immediately go on high alert.

"Go get ready," he adds with a slap to my ass. I jump at the sting. My lady junk catches on fire. "Vixen," he mumbles as he heads for the shower.

I have to confess. If someone had called me that six months ago, I would have called bullshit. But Owen has a way of making me feel sultry, sexy, and a little wicked all at the same time. Simply put, he makes me feel beautiful. It's the reason I wrestle on a pair of skin-tight leather pants and a blouse with an entirely too plunging neckline. Don't worry, I can still dance in this just in case that's what he has in mind.

Did I finally mention we finished those dance lessons? Mrs. Bradford was so moved she presented Owen with a massive basket of baked goods in appreciation. I guess, thanks to him, adult enrollment of her lessons has skyrocketed. We're even considering enrolling in more classes just for fun. There's something I never thought I'd say after finally taking off the tutu I had to wear in elementary school.

"What shoes should I wear?" I ask as he walks into the bedroom.

He's in nothing but a towel wrapped low around his waist. Those two ridges of penis cleavage are just visible above the towel, and I'm here for it.

My gaze runs down to his toes before roaming slowly back up to the smirk on his beautiful face. He's told me he never gets tired of my mentally undressing him. It's a good thing because I don't think I could stop even if I wanted to. And who would want to? The man is one rippling muscle after another.

"Something comfortable and warm," he says.

"What?" What were we talking about? I hear a deep chuckle.

"Shoes. Comfortable. Warm."

"Oh, yeah. Shame on you for muddling my thoughts with all this manhood," I chastise, doing a weird wave thing with my hands. If I'm being truthful, I want to rip that towel off and trace every inch of him with my tongue. "You know, we could just stay here."

"We could," he rumbles softly. "But we're not going to."

"No?" I ask, my fist wrapping in the front of the towel.

"No." He steps closer to me so there's barely an inch separating us. He leans over until his lips brush my ear. "It's your birthday. I'm taking you out to dinner. Maybe we'll do some dancing." His breath tickles my ear, making my body tingle.

"Then I'll bring you home. Strip every inch of these clothes off. Spread you on our bed. Eat you out until you beg me for release." I let out an uncontrollable gasp. I feel him smile against my ear. "Then I'll flip you over, tie you up, and do very wicked things to you all night." He steps back.

"Yes," I say finally. My voice is already hoarse from want. "That." I slap my open palm against his chest. For the life of me, I can't think of anything else to say.

"That," he agrees before moving to the closet. "Any other thoughts you'd like to convey about what your evening holds in store?"

"No. I think you covered everything. Very succinct."

"Good. I wouldn't want you to be confused by anything." He steps out of the walk-in closet wearing a pair of dark-blue jeans. The button-down shirt he's pushing his arms through will highlight his chocolate eyes perfectly. "You about ready?"

"Mmhm," I answer, pulling on a pair of boots. "Wouldn't miss it for the world."

twenty-two

OWEN

I CAN'T BELIEVE how nervous I am. I might be talking a good game, but I'm squirming inside. Everything has to be perfect tonight. Eliot deserves a birthday she'll never forget. I've been working on providing one for a while. You have no idea how hard it is to resist her offer to stay home and get naked.

"You look beautiful in case I haven't told you," I say as I help her with her jacket.

"Thank you. You clean up pretty good yourself." Opening the front door, I let her step through. "What the fudgebucket?" Eliot freezes in her tracks at her ride sitting in front of the house.

I couldn't exactly take her out in the sheriff's cruiser. And who wants to take their own car on a date? So I talked the banker into lending me his classic Mustang.

Eliot takes a step near it and then looks over her shoulder at me.

"Carter lent it to me," I say.

"I'm glad I didn't chalk bomb Carter then."

Carter's sister Cam tends to sell his cars out from under him. He buys a classic wreck; she fixes it up. Then she sells it, and they find the next one. I was lucky his current project was finished and still available. I open the passenger door, extending one arm to usher Eliot inside.

"I feel so swanky," she drawls. I settle her inside and walk to the driver's door. When we're both seated, I pull out a blindfold.

"How adventurous are you feeling?" I ask, waving the blindfold. "I want tonight to be a surprise."

Her eyes narrow. Finally, she sighs. "Fine." I tie the blindfold around her head, making sure it's secure. "If this is just a trip to Sam's for a steak, it's going to be kind of anticlimactic."

"No Sam's. I promise." I fire up the engine and pull away from the curb.

This car doesn't just sound badass; it flies like the wind. I couldn't resist taking it for a cruise after picking it up from Carter. Soon, we're heading out of town. It's not a far drive, but I can't help but open this baby up anyway. I pull off the main road shortly. Slowly, we bump down to the river. I stop on the shoulder in a dirt patch.

"Stay tight. I'll come get you." I climb out of the driver's side. Eliot waits until I help her out of her side. Wrapping an arm around her, I lead her down a trail worn down from generations of feet. Finally, we come to a standstill. I move her in front of me.

"Is this where they'll find my body?" she teases.

"Don't be silly. You know I'd move your body somewhere else. I'm not that much of an amateur." She laughs as I remove her blindfold. It's pitch black around us. "Do you remember how we first met?"

"Of course. You don't forget shooting the sheriff with a firecracker."

"I didn't know at the time that you were working your way through a list of things you wanted to do before turning the ripe old age of thirty. You said you did everything on the list but one. Do you remember what was left?"

"Yeah, but it's hard to have a party by yourself. You need a whole cadre of people."

"Like this?" With a grin, I snap my fingers. This had better work.

I shouldn't have worried. Like clockwork, Reed hits a switch in the dark. The beach is flooded with lights. At least fifty people scream, "Happy birthday!" There are food tables laden with everything anyone could want. A fire is lit in the giant firepit. There are chairs, blankets, coolers full of drinks, and music pumping.

"What?" Eliot's eyes grow wide. Her hands cover her mouth in shock. She spins around to gape at me.

"Happy birthday," I manage to get out right before she throws herself in my arms.

"Best boyfriend ever!" she yells in my ear. We're quickly swamped by people all wanting to hug Eliot. She's laughing and crying as classmates, family, and friends clamor for her attention.

"Nice play, fuzz," Reed says, slapping a beer against my stomach.

"Man, I can't thank you enough for helping me with this," I answer.

"Are you kidding? You're looking at my grumpy best friend hugging people with wild abandon. I would have paid money to be part of this."

"I think we really surprised her, Uncle Owen," my niece says, bouncing up to me. She didn't have a school trip. She spent the day helping Austen and Brontë with the party. The little blonde middle school playboy is standing behind her, looking like he might piss in his pants. "Colton wants to meet you."

"Mr. Steele." He offers his hand. I shake it with a scowl. "Thank you for letting me come."

"Uh-huh."

"Come on, Colton. I'm starving." Tessa drags him toward the food table. Okay, the kid isn't so bad. He has manners, but there's no way I'm letting him get the impression I won't axe murder him and bury his body so deep no one will find him if he makes a move on my niece.

"That boy doesn't stand a chance, does he?" Rand asks, walking up.

"We'll see," I answer. Hey, it's a start.

"Brontë sent me over to get you. They want Eliot to cut the cake, but she won't do it without you there." He walks back through the crowd with Reed and I following.

I had the cake custom-made by Batter-Y-Operated in town. I don't know what is with this town and its sexual innuendo-named businesses. Anyway, it's actually two cakes. One is a three, the other a zero. Get it? It's also covered in candles.

"Thank God, life can continue now," Brontë quips when I step up to the table. "Are we ready?" she shouts. "One. Two. Three." She begins a robust rendition of "Happy Birthday."

When we reach the end, Eliot takes a giant breath. Then she blows the candles out. She has a grin from ear to ear. That makes it all worthwhile.

"Who wants cake?" Austen yells. I back away from the table as it's swarmed. My belly is telling me it needs something from the bar-b-que trailer anyway. It turns out the local FFA teacher cooks a mean brisket. I'm in line when arms wrap around me from behind. I pull Eliot in front of me.

"Hey," I say.

"Hey yourself."

"Having a good birthday?"

"The best," she answers. "You see, I have this guy that chased me all over town until he finally caught me. Now he spoils me rotten by throwing elaborate surprise birthday parties."

"Mmm. Sounds like a lucky guy." She grins up at me. I pull her in for a kiss. A flash goes off in our faces, breaking us apart.

"That one's a keeper," Tessa yells and runs off with Colton in pursuit.

"She's right. This one is a keeper," I agree. I'm not talking about the picture. "I'm really glad I finally caught you."

"Makes it worth shooting you."

"Let's not get crazy."

"Hey, can I steal the birthday girl away for a dance?" Kevin asks, stepping up to us.

"Did you get something to eat?" I ask Eliot.

"Yeah, Austen shoved food in my mouth."

"Then knock yourself out."

With a grin, Kevin takes Eliot's hand. They move to the dance area. I focus on loading my plate. Finding a seat, I watch them dance for a few minutes.

"How was the car?" Carter asks, sitting next to me.

"That thing growls like a wildcat. Thanks."

"Don't thank me. That's all, Cam. She's gifted." His sister sits down across from him. A blush creeps on her cheeks. Soon, we're joined by several others.

I vaguely listen to the conversation as I watch Kevin hand Eliot off to Reed. Rand takes her for a turn, then Arlo. I'd better get out there while she can still remember who I am.

"If you'll excuse me, I see someone I'd like to dance with." Climbing out of the picnic table, I approach the dance floor. I nod at the DJ, and the music changes to a rumba. That's right, I'm about to melt the panties right off of my woman.

"May I have this dance?" I hold out my hand. She takes it. The crowd fades into the background as I pull her against me. The rumba I have in mind is a little less competition and a little more leave her breathless. I move her around the dirt patch like it's our wedding night. This should be something the high school kids aspire to for years to come.

When the song ends, we're greeted by clapping. I pull her against me and kiss her for everything we're worth. The clapping grows louder. Her eyes are slightly glazed when we part.

"We could go home now," she whispers.

"Don't you want to stay at your own party?"

"I'm not much of a partier."

"Okay then. Go say your goodbyes."

Eliot makes the rounds, thanking everyone. No one even seems surprised that we're ducking out early. I'm positive this party will go on just fine without us. I return Carter's keys and snag Reed's. He assures me they can find a ride home. Hand in hand, we head away from the party.

"What about Tessa?" Eliot asks, pulling me to a stop halfway to the truck.

"She's going home with your parents."

"Really?"

"They offered. She's thrilled. Your dad promised chocolate chip pancakes for breakfast."

"Damn, he does make good pancakes."

I get us settled in Reed's truck. It takes a while to get out of the tight parking space, but soon we're on the way home. Eliot is staring out the truck window. I'd love to know what she's thinking.

"Thank you," she says softly.

"For the birthday party? No problem."

"Not just for that," she adds, turning to face me. "I know everyone thinks I've lost my mind the last couple of months. Running around, doing crazy things. But even from the beginning, you were there. You might have gotten irritated by my behavior, but you never gave up on me. It means a lot. You helping me fulfill my insane list means everything."

"It wasn't insane. It was important to you, so it became important to me. You became important to me. I'm not letting you go, Eliot. If that means getting arrested for skinny dipping in the city pool or jumping off a cliff into the river, then I'm all in. Besides," I add, cutting my eyes at her, "I can't wait to see your before-you-turn-thirty-one list."

"Promise I won't scare you off?"

"There's no way you could ever scare me off. If you left, I'd die of boredom." She slides her hand in mine.

"Well, we wouldn't want that."

"No, we wouldn't." We drive in silence for a moment. "Hey, you didn't tell me what you wished for."

"Well, you remember what you told me in the bedroom before we left."

"I do."

"So I wished that, for once, I could convince the sheriff's deputy I'm seeing to break the speed limit."

"That seems like a tame wish," I say, pressing on the gas pedal.

"That's because you haven't seen what I'm wearing under this outfit." She takes out her phone and pushes a photo in front of my face.

"Holy damn," I hiss.

"Yeah, and when you get all this off, I'm going to—" She leans over and whispers in my ear.

"Make sure your seatbelt is tight. We're about to set a land speed record." She squeals when I press the pedal farther.

I don't even know how I'll do half of what she whispered, but if it makes her happy, I'll do anything. I'd even be willing to get shot by a firecracker all over again if it makes Eliot happy.

How can life be this easy? You move to a small town, answer a disturbance call, and the most beautiful woman on the planet falls into your arms. Maybe it wasn't quite that fast, but you know what I mean.

I feel the smile on my face as I snuggle Eliot up against me. If she thinks the first thirty years of her life were good, just wait until the next thirty. I plan to be there every moment. I can't wait to play Clyde to her Bonnie.

ELIOT

"IT'S NOT the end of the world," I assure Owen as he sits on the couch with a scowl on his face. Poor man. He didn't know what he was getting into when he chose to live with two women; one a teenager. "I promise there have been no recorded pregnancies resulting from the seventh-grade school dance."

"You can't possibly know that."

"Trust me, I would have heard about it by now."

He snorts in derision. I roll my eyes.

"Knock-knock," Austen announces, opening the door.

"We're in the living room," I call.

That's how we do it in this small town. You leave your door unlocked when you're home so anyone can waltz in. I know, it doesn't make sense to me either.

"Wow, that's an impressive scowl," Brontë points out as she enters the room behind Austen. "Reminds me of Dad every time any of us had a date. Where is the lucky girl anyway?"

"In her room hiding from her uncle," I answer.

"She is not," he replies.

"Mm-hm, sure. Can I get anyone something to drink?"

"Wine," my sisters respond in unison.

"Bring it to us," Brontë adds. "We need to get the hair started. I assume she's all waxed and everything?" She laughs when Owen's head shoots up. "Just kidding. You might need to do something with that before his head explodes." With a flick of her hair, she heads down the hallway toward Tessa's room with Austen on her heels.

"She's kidding," I assure him. "I mean, who would wax until the freshman dance?" I hear him growl. "Still kidding," I say, flopping down next to him. I pull my feet up under me and throw my arms around his broad shoulders. "Are you really this unhappy I talked you into letting her go?"

"No, not really. I just know the path her mother took. I don't want that to ever happen to Tessa. She's a good kid. A smart kid. But I can't stop worrying that it's somehow hereditary."

"You didn't follow the same path. From what I know about your parents, they are good people. Tessa has more of you in her than you realize," I say. "She also saw what Gwyn's decisions cost her. We've talked a lot about what Tessa wants her life to be. Your sister's life isn't it."

"You have?" He pulls me snug against his chest.

"What else do you think we do in the evenings while you're on shift? It's easier for her to open up to me than risk disappointing her beloved uncle. Now, if I don't head that way with some wine, they will turn on me."

He kisses my temple before turning me loose. Owen is the best kisser. I don't care where they're aimed; everyone is a keeper. I return to the couch with a beer, which he takes happily. Then, with three glasses of wine and a soda on a tray, I head toward the cloud of hairspray emanating from Tessa's room.

"How's it going in here?" I ask, pushing the door open with my hip.

Tessa sits at the dressing table Brontë found at an antique store a couple of weeks ago. She has a grin covering her face as my sister works diligently at her hair.

"We decided on an updo with tendrils," Tessa says excitedly.

"I mean, look at this bone structure," Brontë says. "It should be shown off."

"And these hazel eyes," Austen adds. "I've got just the eyeshadow to make them pop."

"Sounds like you're in good hands," I say. Pulling out my phone, I snap a few pictures. I want every moment captured. "What do you need me to do?"

"Food, El. The princess needs to eat," Austen says.

Tessa giggles. If it keeps her this happy, I'll happily slave away in the kitchen.

"I'm on it."

Fortunately, I loaded up on snackish foods for this very occasion. Returning to the kitchen, I throw some pizza rolls in the oven to heat. I unwrap the container of vegetables and pop open a container of dip. A bowl of miniature chocolate bars is added to the tray. I remember the days of getting ready for school dances. This is far from my first rodeo.

When the tiny pizza rolls are done, I fix a plate for Owen. Don't want hunger adding to his already grouchy mood. Setting it on his lap, I add a kiss on the cheek. Then I'm back down the hallway, laden with munchies. Inside the room, I find Tessa sporting the messiest, most fabulous updo I've ever seen. Brontë has outdone herself.

"Food break," I announce, setting everything out on Tessa's dresser. Brontë adds a little more hairspray to Tessa's hair before letting her up. "I'll grab more drinks." I head back down the hallway.

I'm pouring another round of wine when there's a knock at the door. It must be Rand. He's the only person in this town that refuses to just walk in unannounced.

"Hey, we came for the unveiling," Reed says. He has no qualms about walking right in. "Ooh, do you have more pizza rolls?"

I pour another bag on the cookie sheet and pop them into the oven. Reed saunters into the kitchen to rummage through the refrigerator. Pulling out two beers, he gives me a peck on the cheek.

"When the timer goes off, pull these out of the oven," I instruct.

"Aye, Captain."

He's such a dork. It's probably why he's one of my best friends. Loading the drinks back up on the tray, I leave the men to their own devices. Rand is sprawled in one of the armchairs with Keats happily playing on the floor in front of him.

"Rand, make sure Reed checks on the pizza rolls in the oven when the timer goes off," I say on the way by.

I love Reed, but sometimes the blonde in him kicks in. I don't wait for Rand to answer. This time when I enter Tessa's room, my sisters are sitting in front of her comparing eye shadow.

"Smoky eye with golds and greens," Austen is confirming.

"Definitely," Brontë agrees.

Having a model for a sister is finally starting to pay off.

"Nothing too over the top. No need to send Owen into a heart attack. Oh, and Reed and Rand are here," I say.

Tessa's grin amps up even brighter. She adores her adopted uncles. They dote on her every chance they get. My whole family has adopted Tessa into our brood like she's always been a part of us. I love them even more for that. I hear the front door close. Ten bucks says that's my parents.

"Is G and G here?" she asks excitedly.

She began calling my parents Gpa and Gma a month ago. My dad was over the moon to have a surrogate grand-daughter to impart his wisdom to. Mom just loves that Tessa likes to spend time baking in the kitchen with her when she stays over.

"That would be my guess," I answer.

"I bet Dad brought his camera to snap pictures. It'll be like running from the paparazzi out there." Brontë laughs. "Now stop grinning so we can get your makeup right."

Tessa immediately sobers, which makes my sisters laugh harder.

"You're so beautiful," I say, marveling at the transformation happening in front of me. Not that Tessa isn't beautiful all the time. Her inner beauty made me love her from the beginning. But, this is a glimpse into the Tessa she'll be as an adult. It's absolutely stunning.

"Thank you, Aunt Eliot," she says, blushing.

Soon, it's time for the dress. I took Tessa to buy not just a stunning dress for tonight but new undergarments too. They're a little more than I'd normally let a middle school student buy, but I made an exception. After all, every woman needs lingerie that makes them feel pretty. I have a lot more now that I'm with Owen.

We help her slide the dress into place. She turns for me

to zip it up. Austen grabs my phone and snaps a few pictures of my hands working the zipper up. I fight back a few tears. I hope wherever her mother is, she's getting the help she needs. It should be her here helping her daughter dress for her first formal. I just hope I'm doing a good job as a stand-in mom.

"Shoes," Austen says, helping her step into them.

I also let her pick out a pair of shoes with a slight heel. Nothing crazy. Nothing that will send Owen into orbit. When she's done, I slide a necklace on that I wore to my first dance. It's just a piece of costume jewelry, but it's perfect with the dress. She turns to face us. We take a mass of photos while we "ooh" and "ahh."

"You look amazing," Brontë says.

"Thank you so much, everyone, for tonight," Tessa says. She gives my sisters air kisses like they taught her so she doesn't smear her lip gloss. "Do you think I can talk to Eliot in private for a second?"

"Absolutely," Austen says. "I think I just heard a growl from the living room which means your date just arrived. We'll be waiting to watch you blow his mind."

They leave Tessa's room. She turns to me. I brace for what comes next.

"It should be my mom here doing all of this," she says.

"I know—"

She holds up her hand to stop me. "But she chose something else instead of me. Something more important to her than me. You didn't. You chose me when you didn't have to. Whatever happens, that will always stay with me. To know you opened your home and your heart to me. I'm glad you chose us, Eliot. I'm so glad Uncle Owen knew what he found when he met you."

I grab a tissue from her nightstand. She wraps her arms

around me as I swipe the tears from my eyes. I hug her back hard. I'm glad Owen saw something in me worth loving, and I'm doubly glad he brought Tessa into my life. I'll tell her all that later. I'm too busy blubbering right now.

"You ready?" I finally ask when we part.

"Do you think I am?"

"Absolutely."

"Okay then." She squeezes my hand.

Leaving her room, I'm still wiping tears when I round the corner to a crowd in my living room. My parents did make it, as did Colton and his father. They're visiting with Owen. For once, he doesn't have the scowl on his face that usually is reserved for Colton. The conversation stops when I enter the room. Owen immediately moves to my side.

"Are you okay?" he asks quietly.

I nod.

"Okay, Tessa," I call.

Her room door opens, and she makes her entrance.

"Wow," Owen breathes next to me. "Tessa." All he can do is shake his head.

"How do I look, Uncle Owen?" I can hear the waver in her voice.

"Tessa," he says again.

I hand him my tissue.

"You look like the very best parts of your mom. So beautiful. So grown up." Tessa gives a watery laugh.

"No," Brontë blurts out. "No crying. I'm not spending another hour touching your face up."

She does the trick of breaking the moment. Everyone laughs. Then the pictures begin. Colton shyly presents her with the corsage he's been clutching. He looks like he just won the lottery. In my eyes, he did.

My dad, true to form, takes at least a hundred photos

with his camera. The kids are posed in front of everything under the sun, including several taken in the yard. I've tried pointing out it's already dark, but he assures me his camera can handle it.

Finally, Owen and Justin (Colton's dad) manage to get them loaded into Justin's car. They drive away with my dad in the middle of the street snapping photos.

"I can't believe how old she's getting," Owen says, wrapping his arm around me as we watch the taillights disappear. My family disappears back inside to scavenge the snacks. "Thank you for giving her this."

"Thank you for becoming a part of my life. For bringing Tessa into it."

"We're like a goathead sticker. Hard to get out once it's there. You're mine. I'm not letting you go now. Neither is Tessa." He pulls me into his arms. His warm lips press against mine. "Now, if I can just get these people to go home, we have several uninterrupted hours of wicked naked time."

"Hmm," I say, considering. "We could always slip away to Brontë's and have wicked, naked hot tub time."

"So, a little breaking and entering is what you're proposing?"

"Are you in?"

"Hell yeah, I'm in," he answers with a grin.

Grabbing his hand, we race off toward my sister's house. He pulls me to a stop suddenly. His lips are on mine, his tongue exploring my mouth.

"You never have to ask," he moans when he pulls away. "I'll always be all in."

"Oh yeah?" I ask, pulling away. "You'll have to be fast to catch up with this wild child." I turn and sprint for the hot tub.

"Challenge accepted," he yells.

I smile, hearing his boots racing after me. When did we fall in love, you ask? I think it was somewhere between the firecrackers and jumping off the cliff into the freezing water. Would I change anything? Never, because everything before led me to this place. And this is a pretty damn good place to be.

Owen catches up and sweeps me up into his arms with a laugh. Yep, a pretty damn good place.

Thank you for reading Brazen, book three in the Dansboro Crossing Series. Want more of this steamy small town world? Watch for Peter and Geneva's story coming soon. Get updates and more by subscribing to my newsletter here: https://forms.gle/e7WxDyV4kBKqp81U8

also by avery samson

Justifiable

acknowledgments

I want to thank everyone who helped make Brazen come to life. What you might not know is that a lot of Eliot's list came from things my friends and I did growing up in our small town. I'll always be grateful for those memories. And for the fact the sheriff lived two doors down and never once dragged me to the station. Usually, I just got a stern talking to.

A huge thank you to everyone who read, ARC read, blogged, or shared Brazen. You make this all worthwhile.

As always, thanks to My Brother's Editor for catching my many, many grammar mistakes but still understanding that we small town people have our own way of saying things.

Once again, CJC Photography came through with the perfect couple for the cover. Jared and Jackie make a beautiful Owen and Eliot.

I couldn't do any of this without the invaluable help of Rachel McCarthy. She designed the cover, beta read, helped with story ideas, listened to me whine, and so many other things it's hard to remember everything.

Finally, thanks to my family for keeping me sane. They continue to believe in me and encourage me to keep writing. Without them, I would be lost.

about the author

Avery Samson grew up on a ranch outside of a small west Texas town. Since she could remember, she's had her face stuck in a book. High School graduation found her leaving ranch life for the big city.

After living all over the state of Texas, she now finds herself back on one of the family ranches near Dallas with her husband surrounded by cattle. A lot of them. They're everywhere! When not traveling or reading, she spends her time writing.

Avery would love for you to follow her. She's everywhere (just like those damn cows.)

Join my newsletter for all the latest news.
averysamsonbooks.com/newsletter

Visit my website for my current book list.
averysamsonbooks.com

Join my reader group.
https://www.facebook.com/groups/216191437248096

Like me on Facebook.
https://www.facebook.com/averysamsonauthor

Follow me on Instagram.
https://www.instagram.com/averysamson91/

Watch my videos on TikTok.
https://www.tiktok.com/@averysamson91

Check out my Pinterest page.
https://www.pinterest.com/averysamson91/

Milton Keynes UK
Ingram Content Group UK Ltd.
UKHW010801220224
438165UK00004B/98

9 798224 709328